FALLING INTO ME

FALLING INTO ME

A Novella

Michael Holloway Perronne

iUniverse, Inc.
New York Lincoln Shanghai

FALLING INTO ME

iUniverse books may be ordered through booksellers or by contacting:

iUniverse
2021 Pine Lake Road, Suite 100
Lincoln, NE 68512
www.iuniverse.com
1-800-Authors (1-800-288-4677)

This is a work of fiction. All of the characters, names, incidents, organizations, and dialogue in this novel are either the products of the author's imagination or are used fictitiously.

ISBN-13: 978-0-595-42461-0 (pbk)
ISBN-13: 978-0-595-86795-0 (ebk)
ISBN-10: 0-595-42461-9 (pbk)
ISBN-10: 0-595-86795-2 (ebk)

Printed in the United States of America

*Dedicated to all those impacted
by Hurricane Katrina*

Prologue

Summer 2004

Ever notice how just when you think you have got your life finally going in the right direction, fate steps on all of your dreams? That was exactly how I felt sitting on a plane bound to New Orleans from San Francisco. A flight attendant impatiently stood next to me. She held a mini bottle of vodka as I dug into my pockets for change.

"Correct change is appreciated," the flight attendant said through clenched teeth.

I dug through my backpack for the extra dollar bill. I needed this drink *bad* if I was going to get through this flight.

"All I have is the ten and three ones," I said.

"I'll have to come back later if I get some change," she sighed.

I looked over at my friend, Katie, in the window seat. She snored softly, and I knew better than to wake her. I barely got her on the plane to begin with.

Just when the flight attendant almost rolled the cart down the aisle and left me with nothing more than a Sprite to calm my jittery nerves, the chatty older lady who sat in the aisle seat, and who I had been trying to ignore, piped up. "I have an extra one, baby."

My eyes lit up as she dug into her purse and pulled out a crumbled one-dollar bill.

"Oh, wow, thanks!" I said, perking up.

She gently patted my hand.

"Looks like you need it," she said consolingly.

As I mixed the vodka into my Sprite, the older lady began talking away. I resigned myself to the fact that she had bought herself a few minutes of conversation, even if I was no way in the mood.

"What's your name, baby?" she asked.

She took a tube of light red lipstick out of her purse and started to apply a fresh coat.

"Mason," I answered.

"Are you going home to New Orleans?"

"I live in San Francisco now, but I'm originally from Mississippi. I did live in New Orleans for a few years, though."

She chuckled.

"I knew you were a Southern boy the moment I laid eyes on you. When you helped me put my luggage into the overhead, I told myself, I sure did, that this boy was raised right." She patted my hand again. "I was visiting my niece in San Francisco. I live in Mid-City in New Orleans."

"That's nice," I replied. I had a feeling the next two hours would be pretty long. As the lady continued telling me about her niece's flower garden, her trip to some museum, shopping on Market Street, inquiring how Katie was able to get pink hair and could Katie breathe with that ring in her nose, all I could think about was the fact that in the past few months I had turned thirty, and my whole life had fallen apart. Not because I turned thirty, mind you, although that was tough enough, but because of …

"What do you do in San Francisco?" she asked, forcing me to refocus.

"Photographer."

"Oh, that sounds exciting! What kind of pictures?"

The alcohol began to kick in, and I finally began to relax. Ever since I spent practically the whole time in the bathroom vomiting on a non-stop flight from Puerto Vallarta, I hated flying. Knowing that I would be bombarded by my family with questions about where my boyfriend, Colin, was when I got to New Orleans didn't help.

"What kind of pictures, baby?" she asked again.

"Oh, I'm sorry. The drink's starting to kick in," I said, and she smiled. "Portraits, and I do some photojournalism for a paper there."

"Which one?"

I smiled. I wanted to see what kind of reaction I would get with this one.

"San Francisco Queer Times," I answered.

She clasped her hands.

"That's wonderful!" she exclaimed. "I do love the gays! One of my friends in New Orleans is gay, too. He and his friend throw the most wonderful parties at their condo in the French Quarter. Always such good food. And I'm sure I don't have to tell you, the interior design-beautiful!"

I smiled politely. I couldn't decorate to save my life. That had been Colin's strong point. I looked out the window at the clouds below. Colin. Bastard. God, I missed him so much though, so much my body literally ached at the thought of him. Despite how much he had hurt me, I still couldn't help but miss him. I wished I could slap myself across my face, tell myself to get on with it, screw him, and if he had loved me …

"What's bringing you back to New Orleans?" she asked.

I felt my eyes begin to tear up. I took a deep breath and fought them back. I was not about to lose my shit ten thousand feet up in the air.

"My aunt's wedding."

She clasped her hands again.

"Oh, I do love weddings!" she said. "Wedding cake! There is no better cake in the world than wedding cake. Especially classic wedding cake, white with white …"

As she continued on, my eyes drifted back over to Katie and out the window. Despite all the convincing it took, I was thankful she finally agreed to come with me. Without her support, I didn't know if I would be strong enough to face all of those people. Besides, I felt convinced she had her own demons to exorcise back in the South.

I wondered if my heart could ever heal from any of this. Would I ever be able to shake this pain that had taken a hold of every fiber of my body?

Wait a sec. Let me back up. I'm sorry.

By now, you're probably wondering what the hell I'm talking about. Let me go back to the beginning of my latest drama, or at least, what I would consider the beginning.

It was the day I caught Billy Harris in bed with my boyfriend.

CHAPTER 1

It was 2004. The country wondered what direction the upcoming presidential election would take us, San Francisco's mayor took a lot of heat for issuing marriage licenses to gay couples, and Janet Jackson helped us coin the new unfortunate term "wardrobe malfunction." I was watching the video for her new song when my phone rang.

"Hey, Mace, it's Billy!" an enthusiastic voice shouted on the other end.

I sat straight up on my couch. Billy Harris. *Oh, there's a story!* Billy and I became friends in junior high, and we were practically joined at the hip until we graduated from high school. Billy had also been my first huge crush. I had practically worshipped him. His light blue eyes, corn silk blonde hair, and whiter than white smile made my heart melt every time I laid eyes on him. He also had this charming personality that, combined with his good looks, won people over, or at least I thought so at the time. After graduation, he hightailed his ass to New York City. Over the years, he would pop up every now and then and often disappear as fast as he had appeared. He seemed to drift from one city to the other, pick up a bartending job, and then when he got bored, skip town. His looks, so far, seemed to help him coast along on this path without ever taking on any real responsibilities. You had to wonder how long it could last though. After all, we didn't just recently emerge from the womb. Both of us had turned thirty this year, and his years of hard-core partying were bound to catch up with him.

"Billy, where are you at?" I asked.

"Take a wild guess!"

I half-moaned. With him, who the hell knew? Bangladesh?

"I don't know. San Diego still?"

"Ah, hell no! I haven't been there in months. I was in Phoenix for a while after that. It was just too damn hot-the weather, not the men! I'll be in your neck of the woods soon, man, San Fran!"

"Oh, wow!"

I tried to sound enthusiastic. It's not that I minded seeing him. It's just that Billy has a habit of often stirring up trouble. Of course, he never *intends* for this to happen. It just does. The last time I saw him had been a couple of years earlier. I had lived in San Francisco for a few years at that point. Billy came through town and insisted we had to meet up in the Castro. We hung out for a while, that is until he started hitting on this one cute little Latin guy that ended up having a very worked-out burly boyfriend. One thing led to the next, and Billy ended up getting into a fistfight *in the bar* with the pissed off boyfriend. In all my time, I had never seen a fight break out in a gay bar! After all, gay men would never want to mess up their outfits or their face. Sure, catty words might be exchanged, but blood drawn-never!

The cops showed up, hauled them both off to jail, and I ended up having to bail Billy out. Please keep in mind, at the time, I was barely paying my rent, too.

As soon as he was out of jail, and the charges eventually got dropped, he told me, "Sorry, man, but I gotta get out of here. I'm getting bad vibes from this town."

I wondered what could have brought him back.

"I thought you swore you'd never come back here?" I asked.

"Ah, Mace, that was years ago. I've been studying yoga, and one thing it's helped me with is my fear of letting go. I'm letting the past stay in the past, and I'm embracing my present. Do you know what I mean?"

I didn't really, but I didn't feel like hearing any explanation either.

"When will you be in town?" I asked.

"Tomorrow. I figured I'd hang out for a while, see if I can pick up any work, and then decide what to do."

Flighty, as usual.

"Hey, I got a favor to ask you, Mason."

Here it comes!

"The contact I was going to rent a room from, well he's out of town until next Friday, so I was wondering if I could crash at your place for a few days."

"Oh," was all I could manage to say. I wasn't sure how Colin would feel about a last minute houseguest.

"It'll be like I'm not even there, man. I just need a place to stash my bag and sleep if I don't, well, ya know, get lucky or something," he chuckled.

"I'm sure one night would be okay, but I need to speak to Colin first about something longer."

"No prob, man, I understand. Sounds great. See ya tomorrow. Ah, shit … gotta go. Bye."

"Billy-" I said, before I heard a click. He had never even told me what time he would arrive.

Typical.

The oven timer went off and jolted me back to the present and the surprise dinner I was cooking. It was mine and Colin's six-month anniversary for living together.

Ours had been a whirlwind romance. I had met him a little over a year earlier while we were both taking part in a charity AIDS walk. Right when I felt like my legs were going to give up on me walking uphill in Hayes Valley, Colin appeared with a water bottle and a warm smile for me. Before I knew it, we had progressed from dating, to boyfriends, to living together.

I had recently turned thirty, and I had the boyfriend, a growing career, and wonderful friends. I thought things couldn't possibly get any better.

They didn't.

"Thank God I'm home!" I heard Colin yell as the door slammed behind him. "The phones would not stop at work today."

I heard him walk into our small dining area, and then the footsteps stopped. I knew he had seen the candles lit, the plates set, and the roses on the table.

"Mason? Sweetie?"

He walked into the kitchen to find me standing next to the stove with a bottle of wine in one hand and two plastic wineglasses in the other. A look of panic swept over his face. I knew him well enough to know that he had freaked out and was worried about what holiday, birthday, or anniversary he had forgotten.

"Hey, sexy," I said.

I walked over and planted a deep, wet kiss, the kind he said made him weak in the knees.

"Wow, that's a nice way to come home from work," he said.

He wrapped his arms around me and pulled me tight against him.

"Happy six month anniversary," I whispered into his ear.

"Oh, sweetie," he began, "I'm so sorry. I didn't even think …"

I quieted him by placing another kiss on his lips.

"I just wanted to do something special for you because you deserve it," I said.

I wrapped my arms around him and held him even closer. No matter how bad or long my day may have been, anytime I could hold Colin, kiss him, feel him next to me, it gave my body a tingle, and I automatically relaxed. He brought a calm to my being I had never experienced before. Looking into his bright gray eyes, running my fingers through his sandy blonde hair, feeling his breath against my neck sent me straight to heaven.

His eyes met mine, and he said, "I have the best boyfriend in the whole world, you know?"

"Nah, I think I do," I said.

We both chuckled, our eyes met, and I knew dinner would be delayed.

"Mason, why do you love me so much?" Colin asked.

I raised my head up from his chest and looked at him.

"Why would you ask me that?"

He wrapped his arms around me tighter and sighed. These were the times I enjoyed most-just him and me in *our* bed cuddling and holding each other in *our* home.

Colin's eyes roamed over my uncovered body and his fingertips softly scratched my back.

"I don't know," he began. "Sometimes I just wonder what I did to deserve you. You're so nice to me."

I rose up and kissed him softly on his forehead, his nose, and then his mouth.

"What do you mean? You're a great guy. How could I not be?"

"Thanks," he said.

As I looked in his eyes, I could tell that his mind had wandered off to someplace that did not include me and this moment. I started to ask him more, but I decided not to. Katie always told me I overanalyze too much.

"You're beautiful, you know that?" I said to him.

"Stop," he giggled and buried his face in my neck.

"It's true," I said.

He looked up at me and placed a kiss on my lips. Our eyes met, he smiled, but somehow, I knew he just wasn't convinced.

CHAPTER 2

"It's about time you got here, squirt," Katie said, when I met her for lunch at our favorite burger place off of Union Square the next day. "I was about to start eatin' the freaking menu."

"I'm sorry," I said. "I got held up taking pictures at a koi auction fundraiser for the Gay Men's Health Alliance."

I sat down and started to look over the menu. I'm not sure why because I *always* ordered the same thing.

"A koi auction? As a fundraiser?" Katie said. "Child, you get sent to the most random events to shoot."

"Yeah, well, it's all good experience. I mean, shit, if I can take pictures that make a koi auction look exciting, I can do anything."

She nodded and pushed strands of pink hair behind her ears.

I met Katie at a gay coffeehouse after being in San Francisco for only a week. I remember sitting at a corner table reading a copy of the local gay rag I would later become a photographer for when I heard one of the thickest Southern accents I had ever heard order a cup of coffee. Imagine my shock when I turned around and saw a twenty-something year old Asian lesbian with bright pink hair and a small hoop hung through her right nostril.

She took her coffee and headed to the back of the coffeehouse. I almost burst out laughing when she almost tripped while she checked out a hot redheaded lesbian who played acoustic guitar across the room.

Even though I tended to be shy and reserved, something told me I just had to introduce myself to this girl. I got up and walked across the room to her table. She looked up from some book of lesbian poetry she was reading and said, "Yeah, hon, can I help ya?"

"I'm Mason," I said, and offered my hand to be shaken. "And I'm from Mississippi."

Her eyes lit up, and she said, "Well, Mississippi Mason, why don't you have a seat?"

She then proceeded to tell me practically her whole life story while slurping down her coffee. Turned out Katie grew up in Lafayette, Louisiana, about a few hours from New Orleans. She had been adopted from China as a baby by a prim and proper Southern family that longed to have a child and decided adoption would be the most Christian thing to do. "They just didn't expect their Chinese baby to grow up to be a big ole dyke with pink hair," she laughed.

She said she grew up doing all the things good little Southern girls do—dance classes, recitals, Sunday school, and sweet sixteen parties. "I actually ate out my first pussy the night of my sweet sixteen party. The pussy in question was another sixteen-year-old girl, Betsy Breaux, who lived next door. She told me we could never speak of it, and then she spent the next month on her knees prayin' to Jesus to forgive her. I told her that Jesus had bigger things to worry about than where my tongue went."

Katie said growing up practically the only Asian in town, besides the employees at the King Hu Inn Restaurant, she always felt a little out of place. Her parents forbade her at first to come to San Francisco for school. They had expected her to go to a local college, join a sorority, like her mother, and marry a nice Southern boy right out of college. When she said she told them she was a lesbian and that wouldn't change, in their confusion, they agreed she could go. Now, Katie said she rarely went home, and her parents last visit to San Francisco was all but a disaster.

"For one *thang*, I had forgotten to put away my strap-on before I picked them up at the airport and just left it on the couch. My dad accidentally sat on it," she laughed. "Imagine the look on his face when he reached under his ass and pulled out the eight-inch dong I used on my girlfriend."

I asked her why she had decided on San Francisco.

"I figured between all the queers and the Chinese, maybe I would finally find my people," she said.

I chuckled.

"Have you found your people yet?" I asked.

She sighed, and shook her head no.

"Seems like it's hard for an Asian bulldyke with pink hair and a Southern accent to really fit in anywhere."

But from that day we fit. She became one of my closest friends.

Back to the more recent present. When our food finally arrived, Katie practically attacked her burger. I tried to figure out how to bring up Billy's visit. Katie was definitely *not* one of his fans.

"You won't believe who I heard from," I said.

She finally took a break, looking up from her food. My tone caught her attention.

"Who?" she asked.

"Billy Harris," I answered.

"Not him," she groaned.

"He's going to be in town soon, and he asked if he could crash at my place for a night."

Katie shook her head. "Mason, you know that boy is trouble personified."

"I'll admit that his last visit was kinda crazy."

"Kinda? Crazy?" Katie said, while chomping on a French fry. "He got arrested!"

"Yeah, I know."

"From the moment I met that boy, I could feel that he did nothing but exude negative energy."

"He's only staying for a night. What harm can it lead to?"

"Now why in the hell did you have to go and say that?" Katie said, squirting a mound of ketchup on her fries.

I walked down 16th Street, heading to my apartment in SoMa. I thought about what Katie said. I wondered if she could be right. Would I just invite trouble by having Billy stay over?

My cell phone vibrated in my pocket, and I pulled it out to see the name Savannah flashing on the screen. I smiled immediately. My Aunt Savannah had always been one of the biggest cheerleaders in my life. She was the first person I came out to in my family. To say she was supportive would be an understatement. I also moved in with her right after high school and worked for a while at her drag queen cabaret. Yes, *drag queen cabaret*. Aunt Savannah's theater had been a tourist staple in New Orleans for years, and she was quite the local celebrity. Despite all of her successes, my aunt had never ever been lucky in love, but the tide had finally changed. Colin and I were flying into the Big Easy soon to attend her wedding. If anyone deserved some romance in their life, it was Savannah. I couldn't have been happier for her, and I felt excited to introduce Colin to her and the rest of my family.

"Hey, Aunt Savannah!" I said, answering the phone and stopping in front of a coffeehouse.

"Little Bit," she said, referring to me with the nickname she gave me as a child, "How are things in San Fran? Are you and your man ready for the big trip?"

"I can't wait. I think Colin's a little nervous about meeting the family though," I said.

"You don't worry about that. I'll kick anyone's ass who isn't on their best behavior," she said, laughing.

"How's the wedding plans going? Is the bride getting nervous?" I joked.

"The bride can't wait for her big day! I don't think I've ever been this excited. I can't wait for you to meet Clayton. He's so wonderful to me."

"I'm so happy for you."

"I just wanted to call, say hi, and see if anything is new."

I debated in my head about whether to tell my aunt about Billy's visit. Like Katie, she had never been a big fan of his ... especially after everything with Joey. Joey. He was a whole other story.

I decided. What the hell?

"You won't believe who I heard from!" I exclaimed.

"Whhhhhooooo?" Savannah asked. I could hear the suspicion in her voice.

"Billy Harris. He's coming into town. He asked if he could stay with me and Colin for a night."

Silence.

"Can you believe that? I haven't heard from him since ..."

"The last time he turned your life into a nightmare," she said.

"That whole bar fight was just a big misunderstanding."

There I went making excuses for others again.

"Um, hmmmm," Savannah grunted. "Getting arrested ... you bailing him out ... should I go on?"

I started heading to my apartment again.

"I know. Point taken," I replied.

"Just promise me you'll be careful."

"It's just for one night, Aunt Savannah."

"Okay, okay, enough said. Your mom called me today to let me know when they'd be here."

"I'm looking forward to seeing everyone."

I stopped in front of the steps leading up to my apartment building.

"Clayton's here, sweetie. We have to go to dinner. Kiss, kiss. Call me soon."

"Have fun!" I said, hanging up the phone.

I checked the mail and made my way up the stairs.

"Look who's here!" Colin exclaimed when I walked in.

And there he sat. Billy Harris. He looked blonder and buffer than ever. Thirty seemed to agree with him even more than twenty did. He smiled. His teeth sparkled. Had they been whitened? He stood up, walked over, and gave me a big bear hug.

"Mace! It's so good to see you, man!"

"Yeah, you, too," I said, immediately feeling a little uneasy.

"You've got yourself an awesome boyfriend over there," Billy said, winking in Colin's direction.

"Billy was just telling me a story about an oil worker who blew him in Alaska. It's pretty funny," Colin said.

"Leave it to you to even find a man in the wilds of Alaska," I said to Billy.

Billy put his arm around my shoulder.

"What can I say, huh? The old Harris charm."

"I guess we'll call it that," I said, raising an eyebrow.

"Yeah, I've been all over the place," Billy said. "In more ways than one."

Billy winked at Colin, and I felt my blood pressure rise.

Time to change the subject.

"I wasn't expecting you so early," I said, trying not to sound too put off.

"Yeah, I got here sooner than expected," Billy said. "Luckily, your boyfriend here has helped me feel right at home."

"I tried to spread the Southern hospitality you've told me so much about, Mason," Colin said.

As long as he didn't spread it too much. Wait. Hold up. Why did I even let my mind go there? Colin had never given me a reason to not trust him.

I hadn't been in the same room with Billy for even five minutes, and already, my anxiety level cranked up.

"Good," I said. "I already made dinner reservations for the three of us and Katie."

"Ah, yeah, I can't wait to see Katie," Billy said.

"She's definitely a character," Colin said.

"If you boys don't mind, I'd like to freshen up some and take a shower before dinner. Want to look all fresh for the boys tonight, you know?" Billy said, now winking at me.

"Sure, no problem," I said.

Colin jumped up.

"I'll get you some fresh towels," Colin said, making his way down our hall-way.

Billy turned to me.

"Wow, you look exactly the same, Mace. You never change."

"You either, Billy," I said.

"Hey, Katie, girl! How's it going?" Billy said to Katie, like they were long-lost best friends.

Katie faked a smile.

"I'm good," she said. "*Real* good."

"Right on," Billy said. "Right on."

I had to twist Katie's arm, but finally, she had agreed to meet Billy, Colin, and me for dinner at her favorite Italian place in North Beach.

The place was packed, the smell of their special marinara sauce drifted through the air, and from the sounds of loud laughter, the *vino* was being poured freely.

The hostess led us to our table, and before I could sit down, Billy grabbed the seat next to Colin. Katie shot me a look that included a raised eyebrow, and she tucked stray strands of cotton candy colored hair behind her ear. I pretended not to be bothered by it.

"So, after leaving Alaska, I found myself in some small town in Oregon tending bar at some straight honky tonk type bar to make enough cash to get out of town. Late one night, this hottie comes into the bar. He's around early forties, muscular build, and he had this salt and pepper hair thing that was really working on him. So, as I'm cleaning up and getting ready to close, he's drinking his beer, and I can feel his eyes on me the whole time."

Of course, I thought to myself, Billy always thought every man-gay or straight-was checking him out. If they had a pulse, they must be checking him out regardless of their sexual orientation.

"Then he starts trying to talk to me, asking me how long I'd been in town, was I planning on staying, whatever. I told him I was just working to make some extra cash to get out of town. While we're talking I see his eyes drift down to my crotch."

Colin looked engrossed in the story while Katie stifled a yawn.

"So, I figure what the hell," Billy continued. "I looked down at my crotch and then made eye contact with him. Then I said, 'What? You want some?' The guy looks around the bar and sees that at this point, we're alone. So he goes, 'Hell, yeah. You want to give it to me?"

"Holy shit!" Colin said, his eyes growing wide.

"So the next thing I know, we're in the backseat of his SUV. This mother-fucker gives me some of the best head I've ever had despite the wedding ring on his finger."

Billy paused to dip a piece of bread into oil and vinegar and then pop it into his mouth.

"So a couple of weeks later, I'm leaving town on a bus. As the bus is driving out of town, I see this dude's face on a huge ass billboard. He's the freaking mayor and is running for reelection."

Billy rolled with laughter and a breadcrumb almost fell out of his mouth.

"The mayor?" I asked-skeptical.

"Sure as hell was," Billy said.

"Charming," Katie said.

"Sounds pretty hot," Colin said.

My eyes darted to Colin. Did he just say having some closeted guy in Oregon blowing Billy in the back of an SUV was hot? This coming from Colin, who ranted and raved about how closeted men were the ones that kept gay rights from moving forward.

I noticed how Colin's eyes stayed fixed on Billy. I told myself I was just being paranoid after all the stuff Katie and Aunt Savannah said to me. Colin and I were solid. Billy Harris and his Colgate smile couldn't come between that.

"I'll be right back," Colin said and then headed off to the restroom.

"How long are you staying in San Francisco, Billy?" Katie asked, as if Billy were a disliked in-law who had overstayed their welcome.

"Don't know. Figure I'll see if I can find some work around here, and we'll see how it goes. Might be nice to settle down some place for once."

He looked over at me.

"And I got my good buddy, Mace, here. So, that'd be cool. We can hang out again like when we were in high school."

I smiled. That would be just great, I thought. Then a wave of nausea went through my body.

In the background, I saw Colin walk out of the bathroom and then say hi to someone he knew sitting near the door. Billy glanced over at Colin and smiled.

"You got yourself a really cute boyfriend, Mace," Billy said.

"Thanks," I said, feeling even sicker to my stomach.

Paranoia. That's all there is to it, I said to myself.

"So, do you ever think about settling down, Billy?" Katie asked.

Billy grimaced.

"Nah. I'm too much of a free spirit," Billy said. "I still have a lot of places I want to see and people to do."

He chuckled.

Katie rolled her eyes.

"You talk to your parents lately?" I asked.

The smile disappeared, and Billy's gaze focused down on the napkin in his lap, which he began to rearrange.

"Nah, we don't talk much. They've never liked anything about my life. I really don't try anymore."

I glanced over at Katie, since I knew she dealt with her own parental issues.

"You really should call your mom though," I said. "You know how much she loves you."

"Yeah," Billy said, trying to look more upbeat. "I'll do that. And your family, Mace?"

"They're good. Crazy as ever," I said.

"Aunt still in New Orleans?"

"Yep. Colin and I are going back for her wedding soon," I said.

"Ah, nice," Billy said. "You'll have to tell them I said hi."

"I will."

Colin made his way back to the table and sat down.

"Did I miss anything?" he asked.

Billy put his arm around my shoulder, and Katie let out a little cough.

"Just two old friends doing some more catch up," Billy replied.

The next day at work, I couldn't seem to get motivated to do much of anything. There were no pressing photo assignments at the paper, so I mostly sat at my desk thinking about the way Billy looked at Colin. Productive, I know. I told myself I was just reading into it because of what everyone had said to me.

A new email popped up, and I saw it was from my niece, Lily, who lived back in Mississippi with my sister, Cherie, and her husband, Houston.

TO: MHamilton@gaynewssf.com
FROM: Lily_M@girlmail.com

Uncle Mason,

I'm pissed. No-make that super pissed. Yesterday, I'm on my way to school, and Mom, she goes and freaks out on me all cause I got some eyeliner on. She went on and on about how I'm too young to wear make-up. I told her Stephanie's mom lets her wear make-up, and she told me that's because Stephanie's mom is a whore. Just cause Stephanie's mom wears a lot of jewelry, make-up, and has a new boyfriend every week-that doesn't make her a whore. I think she's kinda cool actually. I don't know why mom is acting so crazy. I'm thirteen now. THIRTEEN! She keeps wanting me to act like a little girl.

What should I do with her?

How much longer until I get to see you?

Love,

Lily

PS—With you and your boyfriend, which one of you faces the sheets? Just curious.

I rolled my eyes over the last question. It was like my niece was thirteen going on thirty. What the hell did she know about facing the sheets anyway? I wasn't about to go into the fact that two men can have sex in the missionary position with her. I bet my sister had quite a handful with Lily, and that humored me to no end. I remember how much trouble she gave our mother at the same age. Cherie was French kissing boys in the huge toy chest in kindergarten.

TO: Lily_M@girlmail.com
FROM; MHamiltion@gaynewssf.com

Lily,

Go easy on your mom. She's always going to see you as a little girl no matter how old you are. It's a mom thing. Trust me. Your grandmother still does the same thing to me, and I'm an old man of thirty. It won't get better. Just learn to deal with it.☺

Colin and I are coming into New Orleans a few days before Aunt Savannah's wedding. I can't wait to see you. I'll bring you back a surprise from San Francisco. No eyeliner though. I don't want your mom to kill me.

Love,

Uncle Mason

PS—It's none of your business who faces what sheets where, young lady.

Just as I hit the send button, my phone rang.

"Hello?"

"Mason, it's Clarissa," a raspy voice on the other end of the phone said.

It was my two-pack-a-day smoking editor in New York. I had recently completed a book of photography on Chinatown in San Francisco. Katie had helped as my assistant, even though she was no more culturally Chinese than me, despite her recent Cantonese lessons.

"Hey, Clarissa. What's up?"

"Looks like we're going to print soon. Looks great, babe, just great."

She paused. I knew she was lighting another cigarette. I had only met her once on a brief trip to New York. The rest of our interaction had all been over the phone and email. But after so many conversations, I had realized that she was always, always smoking or drinking coffee. I wondered how she ever went to sleep at night. But then I wondered if she actually did sleep.

"That's great news! I can't wait."

"So, what's next?" she abruptly said.

Didn't we just finish editing the one book maybe a week or so ago?

"Next?"

"Well, sure, babe. If the Chinatown book hits, they're going to want something else and soon. You start thinking about it."

"Will do," I said.

"Gotta go, babe. Other line. Later."

I had been working so hard on the Chinatown book, and I never stopped to think about what would happen if it were a success. Another book? A wave of panic swept over me. Did I even have another book of photography in me?

Maybe I was just a one-book photographer. Maybe I would never come up with another idea.

Maybe I tend to freak out too early.

Just maybe.

My boss, Barney, a guy around mid-forties with a thing for twenty-something twinks, walked up to my desk.

"Hey, why don't you go ahead and take off? I'll give you a call if anything else comes up to see if you're interested. But I think it'll be a slow next couple of days."

You didn't have to tell me twice. Before Ed had barely walked down the hall, I was making my way down the stairs to the MUNI on my way home.

A recorded voice over the loudspeaker announced, "Four car, Embarcadero, K Line, in two minutes."

Perfect! I had even timed it right for a train that was a straight shot to my neighborhood.

When the train arrived, I hopped aboard. The train was already packed with late afternoon traffic. I grabbed a seat towards the back of the car next to a small old man who snored while his head rested on his chest. How someone could manage to sleep in such an environment was beyond me.

The train took off down a dark tunnel, and I slid back in my seat. I had a few stops to go, so I figured I might as well try and relax. When I got home, I would call Colin at work and see what he wanted for dinner. Billy had said he would already be gone to his friend's apartment by the time I got home.

I looked across the car, startled by what I saw. A guy around my age, with a short fade haircut and of slightly muscular build, smiled at me. Sure, I cruised on occasion, but that wasn't what threw me off for a second. I smiled back, and let my eyes roam down to my lap. I didn't want to give him the wrong idea.

Still, I couldn't help but look up again and take a peek. His resemblance to Joey was uncanny. The same light mocha skin tone, build, dark eyes with long lashes that sparkled, they all reminded me of Joey. Or maybe I was just reading into it. I had been thinking of Joey quite a bit lately.

Joey, now that was a whole other story. While I worked for Aunt Savannah back when I was a teen, I developed a hard-core crush on her stage manager, Joey. He was a year older than me and much more mature. He had been on his own for a few years since his mother, one of Aunt Savannah's employees, died. Savannah had sort of taken him under her wing since his mother's death.

I first met Joey while he worked for my aunt, and my mother and I visited her one summer back when I was just in high school. Even during that first meeting, I felt completely smitten.

"Joey, c'mere for a second, baby," Aunt Savannah called offstage.

I assumed she was speaking to one of the drag queens. Instead, I was surprised to see a guy walk in who couldn't have been much older than me. He was a little taller, a little more filled out, and obviously of mixed race heritage—black and white. He had perfect skin, the color of equal parts coffee and milk. The contrast between his skin tone and his light gray eyes was striking.

I didn't get to look at his eyes long, though, because they darted down when he saw that there were strangers in the room. He looked shy and awkward. He wiped his hands on his pair of worn army pants and avoided eye contact with us.

"Yes, Miss Savannah?" he said, looking up again, but only at Savannah.

"Joey, this is my sister and her boy, Mason," Aunt Savannah said, beaming.

"Hello," he said softly.

Our eyes met, and his mouth turned up in a half-smile.

"This is Joey. He's my stage manager," Aunt Savannah said. She walked over and put her arm around him. "I don't know what I would do without him."

Joey smiled and appeared genuinely pleased at the compliment.

"Nice to meet you," I said.

"Nice to meet you," he said, his voice picking up a little bit.

He had been my first big post-Billy crush. To make matters all the more exciting, he was the first guy to return my feelings. But like a jackass and with the immaturity that came with being eighteen, I let some old lingering feelings for Billy get in the way. He left New Orleans, and from what I heard from Savannah, he ended up living with some cousin in New York. Every now and then I wondered what happened to him. I wondered if he ever thought about …

Ah, shit, my stop!

I jumped up, and made my way to the subway car door. I looked over to where the Joey look-alike had stood. While I had been lost in my thoughts, he had apparently gotten off the subway.

The door opened, and I piled out with a bunch of other people. I raced up the stairs, anxious to get home and start an early weekend.

A couple of blocks later, I made it to my apartment building. I checked the mail-bill, bill, credit card application, credit card balance transfer checks, credit card application, and the new issue of *The Advocate.*

I made my way up the stairs, and I could have sworn I heard noises, voices, coming from my apartment. I glanced down at my watch. Colin shouldn't be home for another couple of hours. I hoped Billy had not brought a trick back to my place or something. That would have been *so* him.

When I got to my door I knew for sure that there were voices coming from inside, and it sounded like one of them was definitely Colin. Maybe he got off early and a friend of his was visiting?

I reached into my pocket and pulled out my keys. A wave of nervousness flowed through my body. I began to sweat, and I could feel my heartbeat start to race. At that moment, I sensed it. No matter how bad I didn't want it to be, instinct told me that what was behind my door I needed to see, but I wouldn't like it.

I started to put the key in the lock, but then hesitated. Again, I told myself I was just being paranoid. I had let the things that Katie and Savannah said get to me. I was just being silly.

I slid the key in the lock and quickly opened the door.

The first words I heard came from Colin.

"Oh, my God!" I heard him say.

I turned to the left, where we had placed our couch. In a moment that I'm sure only took a couple of seconds but felt like ten minutes, I stood in my doorway and stared at the sight in front of me. Colin was naked lying on the couch, and Billy lay on top of him. Billy sat up, naked, except for his socks and a condom on his dick, and he bent down frantically grabbing for his pants.

Colin seemed momentarily paralyzed as our eyes met. Colin was all the way across the room from me, but he had still managed to kick the wind out of me.

"Mace, dude ..." Billy began.

"Shut up," I said softly, my eyes still locked on Colin, who looked too terrified to move.

Billy slid on his pants without even bothering to take the condom off.

"This is nothing, man, really. Just one of those things. It means nothing," Billy said, sounding about as convincing as a used car salesman trying to play off car damages to a customer.

"Shut up!" I said, this time much louder.

I felt my eyes start to tear up, but I willed them to stop. Not now. I could not and would not cry at this moment, not in front of them.

Billy pulled his shirt over his head and slipped on his shoes in what must have been record time for him.

"I'm leaving," Billy said to me.

"Don't you move," I said, my eyes now meeting his. I felt my face flush with anger. I still had not even bothered to shut the door behind me.

Billy took a step towards me.

"Did you not hear what I fucking said?" I screamed at him.

Billy realized I meant business. I actually saw a look of fear, but not guilt, sweep across his face.

Colin finally slowly sat up, and in some weird show of modesty reached over and placed a pillow over his dick as if it were something I, and now, Billy hadn't already seen.

"I'm so …" Colin started to say.

"I don't want to hear shit from you, either," I commanded.

I felt my breathing become heavier as the anger built up throughout every cell in my body.

"Look," Billy said, trying to sound calm. "I really should leave."

"No," I said, looking back and forth between the two of them. "I'm the one that's leaving. Not you. Not him. Me."

I turned, walked out the door, raced down the stairs, out the entrance, and ran out into the drizzly San Francisco summer afternoon.

CHAPTER 3

"Mason," I heard a voice whisper in my ear, and then I felt a soft nudge against my arm.

I slowly opened my eyes, but then squinted them in the unwelcome morning sun streaming in from a nearby window.

"Are you okay?" Katie asked.

I fully opened my eyes and found Katie kneeling down next to her couch, where I had slept the night before.

She held out a cup of steaming coffee for me.

I grunted, groaned, and then finally forced myself to sit up.

"What time is it?" I asked.

"A little after nine. What time did you fall asleep?"

I shrugged my shoulders.

"I don't know. I don't think it was long ago though."

I took the cup of coffee from her hand and sipped the piping hot liquid.

Katie, wearing her Tweety Bird pajamas, silently sat on the floor. I knew she didn't know what to say. She looked as helpless as I felt.

She took her hand and swept her pink bangs out of her eyes and cleared her throat.

"You ready to talk about it yet?"

I sighed. The thought of it made me want to vomit right then and there. I thought how bewildering it was that an emotional scar could make you feel so physically sick. It had been so long since I had felt this way. How could the heart easily forget this pain?

I wanted to toss Katie's spare blanket over my head and hide from everything in the world, but I knew Katie would never let me.

"Why won't you tell me what's wrong?" she asked. "I'm really worried, Mason. You're scaring me."

When I showed up at her place the night before after walking the streets of Hayes Valley for what seemed like hours, I pleaded with her just to let me sleep on her couch for the night. I promised her I would talk to her in the morning.

"I could barely sleep at all last night worrying about what happened to you. You and Colin had a fight?" she asked.

"I wish that was all that it was."

"Then what the hell happened?"

It's not that I was trying to be dramatic by dragging it out. I just didn't know if I could handle the pain yet that would come from verbalizing what I had seen the day before.

"You were right, Katie," I said.

The tears came. I tried to hold them back, but to no avail. This wound went too deep and the pain too much.

"Mason, sweetie …" Katie began.

"Stupid me," I said. "I loved him, you know? I loved Colin all along. But you were right."

"Right about what?" Katie asked softly.

"Billy," I said.

Katie rolled her eyes.

"What did the son of a bitch do?"

"Screwed Colin," I said, finally making direct eye contact with her.

"Motherfucker!" Katie exclaimed and slammed her fist on her coffee table. "Those two sorry good for …"

But then I really started to break down and sob. I covered my eyes with my hands.

"I'm so sorry, baby," Katie said, lowering her voice.

She wrapped her arms around me and gave me a tight hug.

"Yeah, me, too," I said. "I feel like such an idiot. Humiliated. I walked in on them."

"Oh, shit."

"I'm sure Colin didn't expect me to come home early. How could they both …"

I felt myself getting choked up, so I took another sip of the coffee. I could feel the anger begin to rise in me, but I wasn't going to let it win … or let them win.

"Assholes," Katie muttered.

"My boyfriend and one of my oldest friends screwing right there in the living room," I chuckled. "I'm *such* an idiot."

"No, you're not, Mason. Colin's the idiot. Billy's the idiot. Not you. Neither one of them realized how lucky they were to have you in their life."

"I thought Colin and me were solid, you know?"

Katie reached out and placed her hand over mine.

"You'll get through this." She paused. "What are you going to do now?"

"I don't know. I know I don't want to see either one of them."

"You don't have to. You can stay here as long as you want."

She gave me another tight hug.

"Thanks," I said.

My cell phone vibrated on the coffee table. We both looked over and saw the name "Billy" flash on the screen.

Katie reached over and turned the phone off.

"Fuckers," she said.

Three days later, after feeling like I would vomit at any second, I sat at work staring at the computer screen not getting anything done. I knew I should be doing some research for some shoots later in the week, but my mind still could not focus on anything. I had ignored calls from both Colin and Billy for days now. I figured Colin knew I was staying at Katie's. He knew better than to come over there and risk bumping into her. When Katie got pissed, she got *pissed*. Like the time she put the laxative in her boss' coffee because he cut her pay.

I think deep down part of me wanted him to try and run me down, but he didn't.

The phone on my desk rang, and I reluctantly picked it up.

"Hello?"

"Well, there you are! Hell, I was getting worried, boy. I've been trying to get a hold of you for days," Savannah scolded.

"I'm sorry. I've just been swamped lately."

I didn't feel ready to discuss what had happened with anyone in my family, but Savannah wasn't buying it. She could sense trouble.

"Swamped, my ass!" she said. "What's really going on?"

"Just work and …"

"Something's wrong, and you know you'll have to tell me sooner or later."

I looked around the office. Thankfully, just about everyone else had gone to lunch. I didn't want to share my heartbreak with the whole office, too.

"I walked in on something the other day," I began.

I went on to tell her the whole sordid story.

Savannah sat on the other end of the phone in silence taking all of it in. She took a deep breath and then began to curse out both Colin and Billy. After she calmed down, she said, "You know you'll have to face Colin sooner or later. As unpleasant as it may be, you need to confront him to deal with this."

"I know," I said. I just wondered when I would find the strength to do it.

I looked across my desk to the picture Katie had taken of me and Colin last Gay Pride. I picked up the picture, looked at it, and almost threw it in the trash. At the last moment though, I put it in my desk drawer again. As much as I wasn't ready to face Colin, I guess I wasn't ready to completely let him go, either.

After I got off the phone with Savannah, I decided I needed to get out for awhile. I figured a trip to my favorite bakery in the Castro for a slice of triple chocolate cake was in order. The lunch of champions, I know.

I hoped on the L train and took it from Van Ness to the Castro. When I walked out from the underground subway station, it seemed like I was greeted by a sea of couples-couples everywhere! In my head at least, they all walked around, hand in hand, with big smiles on their faces, intoxicated with love.

It pissed me off. No, actually. It pissed me off royally!

I made my way to my favorite bakery on 18th Street. Ernesto, the owner, a mid-forties slightly plump guy, made his way up to the counter when I walked into the store.

"Hey, Ernesto!" I called out.

"Hello, my friend! No time, long see," he said.

"You mean long time, no see?" I said.

"Yeah, yeah," he said, waving his hand around. "What I get you today?"

I placed my hands on the counter, and I tried to slow my breath. I imagined that I probably looked a heroin addict anxious for his next fix.

"I need it, Ernesto. I need it bad."

Ernesto leaned over the counter towards me and cocked an eyebrow.

"You mean the triple chocolate?" he asked in a half-whisper.

"Yeah," I muttered.

Ernesto raised his other eyebrow.

"That bad a day, yes?"

"You have no idea," I answered.

I took my triple chocolate cake and a coffee and picked a small isolated table in the corner that looked out upon the street. I began to dig in, feeling the effect of the sugary goodness immediately. Comfort food is the best.

It is strange how people you haven't seen in years sometimes will start popping up in your mind over and over at certain points in your life. Since this last Billy clusterfuck, I found myself thinking a lot about Joey. I couldn't put all of that one on Billy. I played a part in that dysfunction, too. Billy had been my first big crush, and when I thought he needed me, wanted me, I let myself be blind to what was really going on at the time. Billy had just used me for some sort of self-esteem boost when his own relationship seemed to be going bust. And just when things were starting between Joey and me, Joey walked in on me kissing Billy.

We were just kids at the time, and I'm a realist.

Or a pessimist?

Nothing long term could have come out of something with Joey. We had too much to still learn about life and love. That didn't keep me from taking my Aunt Savannah's convertible and driving to Sherveport, Louisiana because that was where I heard he went.

When I got there, I found out Joey had already been there-and left. A cousin told me he thought Joey was headed to New York. Defeated, I headed back to New Orleans.

I still remembered the sparkle in Joey's eyes though, his gentleness, his …

"Mace?"

I looked up and saw Billy standing next to my table.

CHAPTER 4

"If I wanted to talk to you, I would have returned one of your calls," I told Billy.

He sat down across from me and gave me his best puppy dog sorry look.

"I'm being serious," I said sternly.

"Just give me two minutes," he pleaded.

"For what?" I said, raising my voice.

I noticed Ernesto and a few customers glance over.

"There's nothing you can say or do," I said, lowering my tone.

"I'm really sorry. It meant nothing. It was just sex," he said.

"Just sex?" I said, rolling my eyes. I felt my heart start to race and my blood pressure rise. "You humiliated me, Billy. You slept with my boyfriend! I have a newsflash for you. You don't do that to anyone, much less a friend."

"It just happened. Like I said, it meant nothing, Mace. You can't let it upset you like this."

I stood up from the table.

"You know what you are, Billy?" I asked. But before he could answer, I said, "You're a self-absorbed asshole. You have no respect for anyone, including yourself! I don't even know why I was surprised. It's so you!"

Billy stood up, glanced around the room at the staring patrons, and shoved his hands in his pocket.

"What do you mean, it's so me?"

"If I even have to explain it to you, it's a waste of time."

I started to head to the door.

"I'm leaving town, Mace," Billy called after me. "I'm doing it for you."

I stopped at the door and took a deep breath before turning around to face him eye to eye.

"You've never done anything for me," I said.

I then walked out, and I didn't even get to finish my damn cake.

When I walked into mine and Colin's apartment, the smell struck me first thing. God only knows when he last took out the trash. Scattered throughout the living room were take-out containers, a couple of pizza boxes, and empty soda cans.

"Colin?" I called out.

No answer. I sighed. I hoped he wouldn't be here. I just didn't feel ready to see him yet. Katie tried to convince me to let her come along. I told her I was a big boy, and I needed to do this on my own. Inside though, I was scared shitless. The pain I felt in my heart had not subsided in the least, and I didn't know if I would be able to handle seeing Colin right then. But then, I needed more of my clothes.

I made my way to the bedroom. The bed was unmade, and part of me couldn't help but wonder if he and Billy had …

On our bed!

Couldn't think about it.

I reached up to the top of the closet and pulled out another suitcase. I had planned on packing up just one more bag, but I knew in reality I would have to fully deal with the situation soon. Half, if not more of the furniture was mine, and I had so many personal belongings. It was going to take a moving truck to get everything, and where would I live? There was only so long I could stay on Katie's bumpy couch. I had a cramped neck every morning I woke up there.

"Mason?"

I had been so deep in thought I never even heard him open the front door.

I slowly turned around and our eyes met.

Colin.

Ah, shit.

My stomach did a flip, and I felt my blood pressure shoot through the roof.

"You're home?" he asked. His voice resonated with a hopeful tone.

"I just came to pick up a few more things," I answered.

I went back to my packing as if he weren't even there.

"I was hoping …" Colin started to say.

"Hoping what?" I asked, my voice rising.

"That we could talk so I could explain," Colin said. He dug his hands into his jeans pockets and looked away.

A couple moments of silence went by.

"I do have one question," I said.

"What?" he asked, looking up.

"Why?" I said, my voice breaking.

"I don't know," Colin said, shaking his head.

"You don't know why you fucked around on me? And not just with anyone, but my oldest friend?" I yelled.

I haphazardly threw some more clothes in the suitcase. Suddenly, I just wanted to get the hell out of there.

"It just happened all so fast," Colin said, tears falling down his cheeks. "Maybe I needed to test myself."

"Test yourself?" I spat.

I started zipping up the suitcase. I didn't want to hear any more of it. Nothing.

"Everything with us, it just happened so fast. I think part of me needed to do it to figure out how I felt. I know now, Mason. You're the one for me."

I chuckled. I always laugh inappropriately when I'm angry or sad.

"You had to fuck Billy to figure that out?"

I pulled the suitcase off the bed.

"Mason, I know I screwed up, but I know now for sure. You're the one I want."

I took a deep breath, and I tried to calm myself down.

"You know how I'll know when I've met the right man, Colin?"

Colin shrugged his shoulders.

"When he doesn't have to do what you did to figure out I'm the one for him."

I walked past him into the living room and towards the front door.

"I'm not giving up," I heard him call after me.

Once I made it outside, I let myself do it. I let the tears fall. But only then.

Katie and I sat on a bench in Golden Gate Park eating caramel corn and watching the fog drift through the San Francisco Bay. One of the first things I did when I moved to San Francisco was come to see the Golden Gate Bridge. After so many years of seeing it on television and movies, it made my arrival in town sort of complete. I was really here in the gay mecca of the United States. Little Mason Hamilton from Andrews Springs, Mississippi had made it to the other side of the country. So, lately whenever I found myself at a crossroads, I would take the transit here to the park to sit, look at the bridge, and contemplate.

"I was so looking forward to taking Colin back home to meet my family, you know?" I said.

Katie reached over and squeezed my hand.

"I know," she said softly.

She motioned towards the popcorn to ask if I wanted more. Not even my favorite caramel corn could soothe the heartache.

"I don't know if I even feel like going back now," I said.

"You have to go, Mason. You've been looking forward to it so much. And you know how much it'll mean to your aunt."

"I know. I shouldn't let this stop me. It'll just be so hard going back with all of the questions or the looks of sympathy because my boyfriend screwed around on me. It's humiliating. I know I should be able to, but I just don't feel like facing it by myself."

"It's important to you though ... to be there for your aunt."

Suddenly, a thought crossed my mind.

"I have an idea!" I said, turning to her with a raised eyebrow and a sly smile.

Katie swallowed a mouthful of popcorn.

"Why do I feel scared to ask?" she said.

"You can come with me!"

"Me?" Katie said, pointing to herself.

"Well, yeah, you! You can visit your folks in Lafayette while we're there, too. Come on, Katie, when was the last time you went back to the South?"

"Forever, and for good reason, ya know!"

"I'm sure your parents would love to see you."

"I'm not so sure after the last visit."

"Yes, they would. And it would make me feel so much better to have my good friend there with me. The ticket is already bought. I'll just have it changed to your name. Come on! How can you pass up a free trip to the Big Easy?"

"Well...."

I could tell I was wearing her down.

"Think of how much fun we'd have in the Quarter, the food, the daquiries," I smiled.

Katie twirled her pink hair around one of her fingers. She sighed.

"You and me in New Orleans, Mason? I don't know. Sounds like craziness."

"Fun craziness!" I said.

"Oh, what the hell. Okay."

I gave her a big hug and a kiss on the cheek.

"We're going to have a blast," I told her.

CHAPTER 5

"Thank God. I thought I would vomit," I said to Katie, right after the captain announced that our plane had begun its descent into New Orleans.

Katie, having just woke up, yawned and rubbed her eyes.

"I can't believe I'm back in Louisiana," she said. "To be honest, I'm not sure I'm really up for seeing my family."

I swallowed the last of my cocktail I had needed to calm my nerves during the flight.

"Come on, Katie," I said. "You have to see your family while you're here. Especially after their trip to San Francisco."

"After that last disaster of a visit?" she said, before gazing out the window and looking at the swampland below.

"That's exactly why you *should* meet with them," I replied.

The little old lady that had given me the money for my cocktail reached over and squeezed my hand.

"You made it through, dear," she smiled reassuringly.

"At least the flight part," I said.

She raised up slightly and looked over at Katie. I saw her gaze focus on Katie's nose ring.

"Dear, how do you get that thing in your nose?" she asked Katie.

As soon as Katie and I made it down to baggage claim at the New Orleans airport, I heard Savannah scream out, "Little Bit! Over here!"

Savannah made her way over in her classic short skirt and high heels. Her blonde hair was up in a French roll. Her make-up-flawless. Even now that she neared sixty years old, she was beautiful and looked nowhere near her age.

I dropped my bags and threw my arms around my aunt and hugged her tight.

"It's so good to see you, Aunt Savannah," I said.

"You are a wonderful sight for this old woman's eyes," she said, looking me up and down.

"You and old should never be said in the same sentence," I told her.

She playfully slapped my arm.

"It's nice to see that the big city hasn't taken your Southern gentleman qualities away," she said.

"This is my friend, Katie," I said, motioning for Katie to walk over.

Savannah immediately gave her a huge hug, which I think caught Katie off guard.

"I've heard *so much* about you, girl," Savannah said.

"You too," Katie said.

Savannah pulled back and looked Katie over.

"And this hair," Savannah said, running her fingers through Katie's pink locks. "I absolutely love it! It's just fabulous!"

Katie laughed and said, "Thank you!"

I picked my bags back up, and Savannah put one arm around Katie and the other one around me.

"Now, I know the two of you must be starving after that flight. We'll take you back to my place and fill both of you up with some good down home cooking," Savannah said.

"You cooked?" I asked.

"Hell, no!" Savannah said, laughing. "I had take-out from Belinda's delivered."

As we drove through the streets of New Orleans-Airline Highway, Claiborne, Canal, and then finally into the French Quarter, I found myself flooded with memories from the past. In a way, it felt like it had been forever since I walked along these streets as a teenager. But it some ways, it seemed like it was yesterday and I had never left.

Katie sat in the back of Savannah's red Mustang convertible and the two of them had gotten into a deep conversation on the merits of fried shrimp versus fried crawfish. I began to think that Katie had begun to loosen up and was actually happy to be back in Louisiana.

While we were stuck in the French Quarter gridlock on our way to Savannah's house, I wiped the sweat from my forehead.

"Not used to the humidity any more, huh?" Savannah chuckled.

"It's a little overwhelming," I said.

"Shit, it's so muggy," Katie said, looking pale.

As we drove down Dauphine Street past restaurants, bars, and shops I remembered, I took a deep breath of the hot humid air. The smell of seafood cooking nearby drifted through the air. Partiers, carrying cocktails in plastic "go cups," sauntered down the sidewalks. No one, anywhere, seemed in a rush. It felt good to be home.

"This is the new guesthouse," Savannah said, pointing to the charming little cottage that she had built in the courtyard of her French Quarter house. From the outside, all passer-bys saw were dark brick walls. But once you walked past the wrought iron gates, just like many French Quarter homes, you were transported to what felt like another world from the hustling busy streets of the Quarter.

Inside, Savannah had a huge courtyard with many tropical plants, a well-manicured flower garden, and a flowing fountain with an angel sculpture in the middle. Her courtyard was still the tranquil place I had spent many lazy afternoons in as a teenager.

"It's nice," I told Savannah, as I peeked into the windows of the guesthouse.

"I thought you and Katie might enjoy staying in it. The first official guests to do so," Savannah said. "Come on in."

She opened the door, and we followed her in and dropped our bags inside. The living room included a daybed with a fluffy oversized white comforter, a small kitchen table, and an entertainment center filled with the latest electronics.

"The bedroom is in the back. I'll let the two of you decide amongst yourselves who sleeps where," Savannah said. "And the fridge is already packed with goodies, including some Jax beer.

"Well, this must be Mason," a booming voice said from the front door.

I turned around, and immediately knew it must be Clayton.

"And this," Savannah said, walking up to him and throwing her arms around him, "is the love of my life."

She planted a big-and deep-kiss on him that went on for quite a while.

Katie and I looked at each other. We weren't sure if we should leave them alone for a while.

"Now, honey, we don't want to shake the young kids up by having them see the old folks all lovey," Clayton chuckled.

Clayton stood a good foot taller than Savannah, even with her heels. He was a very handsome, distinguished-looking man with his striking snow-white hair and beard matched with a still-youthful face. His shoulders were as wide as a linebacker's. And most importantly, he looked at my aunt with eyes full of devotion.

"Oh, trust me, I've seen a lot more," Katie said. "So, you go right ahead."

"Sounds like a challenge!" Savannah laughed.

She took Clayton's hand and walked him over to us.

Clayton stretched out his hand.

"Good to finally meet you, Mason," he said. "Your aunt has told me so much about you."

I gave him a firm handshake.

"Likewise."

He turned to Katie

"And this pretty little thing must be Katie," Clayton said, taking her hand and kissing the top of it.

Katie, the big activist lesbian, actually blushed and giggled like a high school girl who just had the school quarterback say hi to her.

"Nice to meet you," she said.

Clayton wrapped his arms around Savannah.

"I'm so glad both of you could be here for the wedding. We're going to have a real party," he said.

I looked over at my aunt. A twinkle shone in her eye that I had never seen before. She glowed and looked completely content. She had always had a jubilant personality, but I had always sensed an underlying sadness. Now, that sadness had been replaced with joy, and I couldn't be happier for her.

"I can't tell you how happy I am to be here, too," I said.

I sighed a deep breath. For the first time in a very long time, I felt myself relax.

After briefly unpacking and a rest period, Katie and I took off for Bourbon Street. We figured that Savannah and Clayton wouldn't mind a little alone time.

Sunday afternoon was happening on the street. The street had been closed off to traffic for the weekend, and partiers made their way down the street, drinking alcohol and then more alcohol.

Katie had only been to Bourbon a couple of times as a teen since she grew up in Lafayette. On Bourbon Street, Katie and her pink hair and piercings rarely got the stares she otherwise sometimes did in San Francisco. There were much more colorful characters on the Bourbon Street, many of them in drunken abandonment.

We slowly made our way down the street, caught in the sea of people. On each side of the street were bars, more bars, strip clubs, souvenir shops, restaurants, and the ever-popular daiquiri shops that often had more than fifty flavors of frozen daiquiris. Many often served pizza by the slice, although food often felt like an afterthought along this street.

"How's it feel being back?" Katie screamed into my ear, attempting to be overheard over the blasting music coming from a nearby karaoke bar where a young woman sang a dreadful version of "These Boots Were Made For Walking."

"Sort of surreal. It feels like such a long time since I ran these streets when I lived with Savannah, but in some ways, it all feels like yesterday."

We made our way to the invisible wall that separated the straight and gay sections of Bourbon. Locals referred to it as the invisible wall because drunk straight tourists would stop abruptly at the intersection of Bourbon and Saint Anne sensing that something was different on the other side of the street. Maybe it was the practically naked strippers often on top of the bars inside, who bobbed their dicks up and down underneath a tiny cloth.

"You should do some photography while you're here," Katie suggested.

I felt my cell phone vibrate in my pocket. I pulled it out and saw Savannah's number flashing on the screen. I motioned to Katie to follow me onto Orleans Avenue, which was always a tad bit quieter.

"Hello?" I answered, putting a finger over my other ear to try and block out the sounds from the street.

"Guess who I just heard from, and they're coming to the wedding?" Savannah screamed on the other end.

I assumed it had to be some sort of Hollywood celebrity. Savannah had met and befriended quite a few actors who would come to town on location shoots.

"I have no idea."

"Joey!" she shrieked on the other end of the phone.

I almost dropped the phone right then and there.

"Joey?" I repeated.

I moved further from Bourbon to Royal Street so I could hear better.

"I found him on the Internet a couple of months ago. He said he was going to try and make it down, but he needed to see if he could get off work. He's going to be here! Isn't that exciting!"

I stood there speechless.

"Mason, are you there?" Savannah said.

"Wow, that's great!" I finally said. "It'll be great to see him again."

"Got another call, Little Bit. Let me know when you two would like to have dinner."

I heard her hang up.

I looked over at Katie, who gave me a strange look.

"You look like you just got some messed up news," she said.

"Joey is going to be here for the wedding," I said, still trying to digest the information.

"Joey? The guy you had the thing for when you lived here?"

"Yes," I said.

Katie laughed.

"Hey, this is great! Maybe it's exactly what you need right now. You know, rekindle an old flame."

I shoved my phone back in my pocket and looked around. I felt disoriented all of a sudden.

"Nah. I mean that was so long ago. We were just kids back then."

"Hey, can you keep an open mind? Geez!" She grabbed my hand and pulled me back toward the bars.

As Katie led me back into the crowd and towards the crowded gay video bar, the Bourbon Pub, I wondered if she could be right. Would any of those old feelings resurface? Could it be possible after so many years?

CHAPTER 6

Katie decided she needed a nap after we unpacked. God only knows why, since she slept during the whole flight. I didn't argue since I figured some "me time" back in the Big Easy might help my mood-and calm my nerves.

I took out my favorite camera and decided to take some shots. I first developed my love of photography when I lived with Savannah. She gave me an old thirty-five millimeter camera she hadn't used in years. On a whim I went out and bought a few rolls of film and just started shooting throughout the French Quarter. With its historical architecture and eccentric citizens, it proved to be a great training ground for a budding photographer. Savannah noticed my interest and offered to pay for some photography classes at Delgado Community College. Everything started rolling from that point.

I headed down Royal Street, where many of the Quarter's oldest shops were located. There were the usual tourists and antique shoppers strolling down the street, along with a few hustlers asking for spare change on the corners.

The soulful sounds of jazz music drifted through the air from the street performers around Jackson Square. Maybe I was on an unexpected high from being home, but I could swear I even smelled the beignets, French style donuts minus the hole, cooking at the nearby Café Du Monde.

I immediately started snapping away with my camera: a tap dancing boy on the corner of Royal and Bourbon, an all gold mime standing on a box, a couple of Japanese tourists looking captivated while riding a horse and buggy through the Quarter. I had felt stalled on my creativity ever since I found you know who screwing you know who; however, now I felt energized.

After taking close to a hundred pictures with my digital camera, I walked back to Savannah's theater. I walked up to the theater on Orleans Avenue, which looked the same as it did when I had worked there so many years before. The exterior was still the same, painted in black with a simple sign hanging above that read "Savannah's". Next to the door hung a sign advertising the box office hours. Savannah, through her drag queen cabaret, had become a local celebrity. Many tourists were told that their trip to the Big Easy wasn't complete without seeing one of her shows filled with outrageously costumed female impersonators. Savannah always hosted most shows and entertained the audience with her bawdy sense of humor.

When I walked through the front door, I immediately saw Savannah speaking with a well-dressed man, probably in his early forties. His eyes darted all over the room as Savannah spoke to him.

"I had all the wiring in the lobby replaced just this last year," she said to him.

She turned around when she heard me walking toward them.

"Mason!" she exclaimed. Her expression reminded me of a five year old that had just gotten caught after eating a box of chocolates before dinner.

"Hey, what's going on? I thought I'd stop by on the walk back to your place," I said.

"This is Mr. Butler," she said hurriedly, as if she had just remembered her manners.

"I'm Savannah's nephew, Mason," I said, extending my hand.

He shook it, strong and firm.

"Bob Butler," he said. He glanced down at his watch. "If you'll excuse me, I have another appointment with an investor."

"Of course," Savannah said. "I'll look forward to speaking with you soon."

"Nice to meet you," Butler said before leaving.

"Who was that?" I asked.

I was dehydrated from the humid August New Orleans air, and the camera hanging around my neck began to weigh heavily.

"Sweetie, you're all bright and red. You need some water."

She walked over towards the lobby bar.

"And you're avoiding the subject," I replied, but still greedily grabbed the bottle of water she offered to me.

"Just some business deals," she said, hesitantly. "Ah, shit. I don't know why I'm scared to tell you."

"Tell me what?" I asked.

She walked over and grabbed my hands.

"I'm planning on selling the theater," she said.

"Selling the theater!"

I couldn't believe what I had heard.

"Sweetie, I'm not getting younger here," she said, inching her mini skirt down.

"What are you talking about? You're in as great a shape as ever."

"I've been working hard for a long, long time. And now that I'm marrying Clayton, I want to take some time to relax and just enjoy life. Travel. See more of the world. Spend my afternoons shopping at Saks."

"That just doesn't sound like you though," I said.

I turned around looking over the entire lobby. The walls were adorned with pictures of Savannah and her various performers. A framed "New Orleans Businesswoman of the Year" award hung near the entrance.

"You're so much a part of the place," I said, shaking my head. "You're part of the Quarter."

She sighed.

"I've had so many good, no, make that wonderful years here. Hell, it's been a blast. I've loved being on that stage and working the audience. I've even enjoyed dealing with these drama filled drag queens. They've become my family, you know."

"What will they all do?" I asked. Some of Savannah's performers had been with her for more than two decades.

"You won't believe how much I'm getting for this place. Between my savings, the sale, and Clayton's own money, we'll live comfortably the rest of our lives. As far as the girls," she said, gazing at one of the latest group photos on the wall. "I'll be able to give each one of them a *very nice* severance. They won't have to worry about anything for quite a while."

"Wow, I'm just …" I started to say. "I don't know. I never expected this."

She gave me a tight hug.

"What do I say about the dice?" she asked me.

"Sometimes you've got to roll them. See what happens," I said reluctantly.

"It's life, Little Bit. Change helps keep our lives from growing stale. We have to accept and welcome it. I think I'm ready for some new adventures, and I can't wait to experience every one of them with Clayton."

I felt myself tear up. "I just want you to be happy."

She wiped away a lone tear that had managed to escape my right eye.

"And I am, baby. I'm so happy," she said and then paused. "And don't you worry, Little Bit. I know you've had a real hard time lately. But Aunt Savannah is going to help make it better."

"And just how do you plan that?" I asked, laughing.

"I always have before, haven't I?"

"Yeah, you have," I agreed. "But this time is different. I don't know if I'll ever be the same."

"I know what's in here," she said, placing her hand over my heart. "You're going to be okay."

I couldn't help it now, and the tears began to flow freely, and Savannah gave me another hug.

"I love you, Aunt Savannah," I whispered into her ear while she held me.

"Thank you all so much and have a fantastic night!" Savannah announced to her audience after the night's show.

Katie and I made our way backstage afterwards. She had been blown away by the performances of all of the drag queens and the elaborate costumes, especially Savannah's showstopper, Miss Althea. Miss Althea had been performing at Savannah's for almost twenty years. I knew better than to remind her of that since she felt it would date her.

As soon as we made it behind the curtain, amongst the scattering performers, I heard a deep voice bellow, "Well, look a there!"

I recognized the voice immediately.

Katie and I turned around to see the spectacular sight that is Miss Althea. Despite being, I guess, well close to sixty, her cocoa skin was as smooth as the last time I had seen her years ago. She wore a huge bright green ball gown and carried a silver parasol.

"Miss Althea!" I exclaimed.

She ran up and playfully slapped me across the arm with her parasol.

"Well ain't you just getting handsomer by the years! Um, um, um!"

She looked me over from the top of my head down to my shoes.

"Thank you," I said.

Her attention turned to Katie.

"And who is this sweet child with the cotton candy hair?"

"Katie," Katie said. "I loved your rendition of "Endless Love.""

"Your friend has nice taste," Miss Althea said to me. "Miss Katie, I hope to get to know you better while you're visiting our beautiful city."

"I'd love that," Katie said.

"There you are! I see you already found Althea," Savannah said, walking up and putting her arms around both Katie and me.

"She's always hard to miss," I said.

"You got that right!" Miss Althea said. She turned her attention back to me. "Where's your *huzzband* you were supposed to be bringing?"

An uncomfortable tension overwhelmed the room. I could feel both Katie and Savannah's eyes on me ... both of them not sure what to say.

All of those feelings of hurt and disappointment washed back over me like a large violent wave crashing on a peaceful beach.

I tried to shrug it off. "Long story, but he's not in the picture anymore."

"Oh, Miss Althea just stuck her well-pedicured foot in her mouth! I'm so sorry."

"No, biggie," I said. I tried to smile, but it was a sorry ass attempt.

Awkward silence.

"Well, this girl has to go take care of some *bizzness*. Too much chicory coffee before the show."

And with that Miss Althea scurried off.

"Who's hungry?" Savannah asked.

I raised my hand.

"Me, too. Starved," Katie said.

"I think a trip out for dinner is in order!" Savannah announced.

"I can feel the heartburn already," I said.

Savannah, Katie, and I met Clayton out at Belinda's, one of Savannah's favorite restaurants in the Quarter. Plate after plate of delicious, and heart attack causing food, got delivered to our table. Fried catfish, homemade mac and cheese, fried okra, and hushpuppies were just the starters.

Katie eyed all of the food suspiciously.

"At this rate, I'm going to gain ten pounds before I go back to San Francisco," she said.

Savannah and Clayton chuckled while piling their plates high with food.

"Katie, girl, you can't tell me you don't miss some of this good Southern cooking!" Savannah said.

Katie scooped a small spoonful of mac and cheese on her plate.

"I think it's safe to say I've been detoxed by this point, but here goes," Katie said, before taking her first bite of true Southern food in years.

"Aunt Savannah, how do you eat all of this and still keep that girlish figure?" I asked.

"Honey, you try herding groups of drag queens around every night! You'll work it off," Savannah said.

"I think it's that your aunt just can't help but be beautiful," Clayton said.

My aunt and Clayton locked puppy dog eyes and then kissed.

"You two are so sweet," I said.

"Well, we try, Little Bit," Savannah said.

Despite my protest at all of the calories, I had to admit that all of the food tasted delicious. It was if every bite of food brought me back closer to feelings of down home warmness.

As we finished our slices of banana cream pie for desert, Savannah said, "Mason, your mom, sister, Houston, and Lily will be here in a couple of days. I booked rooms for them at the Bourbon Orleans."

"It'll be great to see everyone," I said.

She reached over and took my hand.

"I wish Elvis could be here," she said, referring to my father, who had passed away the year before.

"Yeah, me, too," I said.

That trip back home last year for his funeral had been rough on me. Colin had been the one to help me with my grief at the time.

"But we know he'll be there in spirit."

I nodded.

"So is this where the party's located?" I heard a somewhat familiar voice say. "Miss Althea said I could find you here."

Everyone turned around, and there he stood. He looked more handsome than what I even remembered. He looked a couple of inches taller, more filled out, with the slightest hint of stubble on his face. There was a new level of confidence and maturity in his aura.

"Well, look who's here!" Savannah said, jumping up and giving him a hug.

Our eyes met. As cheesy as it may sound, it felt like I had been transported back to 1992, and I felt butterflies in my stomach.

After all these years, it was Joey.

CHAPTER 7

"You look fantastic!" Joey said to Savannah as they embraced.

I felt Katie kick me underneath the table, and she shot me a look that I read as saying, "Get up and say hi, dipshit!"

I got up and walked over to him. I sensed a little awkwardness coming from him, too, as I made my way over. Then his facial expression relaxed, and a warm smile spread across his face.

"Hi, Mason," he said.

I immediately put my arms around him and gave him a tight embrace. I wanted him to know that all of those years ago, I did care about him-a lot.

While we hugged, I felt his arms pull me closer to him as if to tell me that all had been forgiven.

My mind drifted back to the night of our first kiss, when Joey had saved me from myself after my first night of hard drinking.

"So how come you don't have a boyfriend?" I sort of slurred.

He laughed, and I could have sworn he pulled me in tighter as we walked, our pace slowing.

"I guess the right guy hasn't asked me out yet," he said.

"But you're so damn cute!" I said.

Alcohol—the number one truth serum.

We walked by a drunken old guy wearing an LSU sweatshirt who sat in the doorway of someone's house singing the country song "All My Exes Live in Texas." I was glad for the distraction because I couldn't believe what I had just said. Yeah, I had thought it, but I normally would never have had the nerve to just come out and say it.

As we neared Savannah's, Joey said, "Wow, so you think I'm cute, huh?"

I felt myself beginning to sober very fast. My drunken mind went into overtime trying to figure out a proper response.

"Well, yeah. I see guys hit on you or check you out all of the time when we're out, but you never do anything about it."

"I guess …" Joey paused as we reached the door that led to Savannah's. "I've been thinking a lot lately. Clearing my head, you could say."

Clearing my head? I tried to decipher that one, but I wasn't sure what it meant. Why couldn't guys just say what they mean?

Funny, coming from me!

"Oh, okay," I said. I dug into my pocket for my key.

"But, I …" he started to say. He shuffled his feet on the sidewalk.

"Yeah?"

"I think you're pretty cute yourself," he said.

I can only imagine how many shades of red I must have turned. I was so damn transparent sometimes.

"Really?" I said.

Why couldn't you just say thanks?!

"Yeah, I do," he said, looking me straight in the eye.

Finally, I said, "Thanks."

We had another little awkward moment. We were both waiting for the other to say something first.

At last, he put his arms around me and gave me another tight hug—one that lingered for a moment. His arms wrapped around me again made me want to melt. He stepped back, and I found myself getting lost once again in his eyes.

"I guess I better go in …" I began.

But then he pulled me closer to him and kissed me on the lips, gently at first, but then more passionately. I felt myself relaxing as my lips parted and his tongue slowly entered my mouth, caressing mine. I wrapped my arms around him and returned his tight embrace, feeling the muscles along his back.

It was freaking electric!

When he pulled away, I took a moment to compose myself, and he reached down and took my hand.

"I'll let you go get some rest. Maybe we can talk about all of this later," he said.

"Oh, yeah. Sure. You bet," I said, sounding like a dork.

He gave me one last peck on the cheek, and he watched me open the door.

"Night," I said.

"Goodnight," he said, before he walked away.

I shut the door to the courtyard behind me, and then I fell back against the door. I was in sheer heaven!

I could feel Savannah, Katie, and even Clayton's eyes on us as Joey and I hugged. I finally pulled away.

"It's so great to see you," I said.

"You, too, Mason. Real good," he said, our eyes never parting.

"Well, are you hungry?" Savannah asked.

Joey eyed a tray of fried chicken that a waiter delivered to a nearby table.

"Honestly, I'm starving," he said.

"Belinda, honey!" Savannah called out to the proprietor of the restaurant, who was sitting at the bar and watching the evening news.

Belinda turned around.

"Yeah, baby?"

I took a good look at Belinda. How was it possible that she looked the same after all of these years, too? Was it the humidity in the air?

"Can you bring this boy here a big helpin' of some real food? He's been starving up in New York," Savannah said, putting her arms around Joey.

"Oh, you know I can hook him up," Belinda said, making her way into the kitchen.

"I've just got to give you another hug!" Savannah said, embracing Joey. "It's so good to have both of my boys home."

Joey looked at me over Savannah's shoulder.

"It's good to be home," Joey said.

"This is my good friend, Katie, from San Francisco," I said.

He walked over and immediately gave Katie a big hug despite having just met her.

"I'm looking forward to getting to know you," he said.

"You, too," Katie said.

She glanced over at me and smiled.

And I spent the rest of the meal not able to take my eyes off of Joey. He spoke of his life in New York working in social services, his new admiration for real Italian pizza, subways, and skating every winter at Rockefeller Plaza.

"So, Joey, how does it feel to be back in the Big Easy after so long?" Clayton asked.

"Well … it's a little surreal. It feels like it's been a lifetime ago, but then …" he said, glancing at me. "It feels like only yesterday I was only a kid running the streets of the Quarter."

He paused.

"It reminds me a lot of my mom," Joey said, trying to smile.

Savannah reached over and patted his hand.

"I miss your mama every day to this very day," Savannah said, of the long-time friend who also had worked for her. "And she loved you so much. You were her everything."

Joey's eyes lit up a bit when Savannah said this. I wished that I had gotten the chance to meet Joey's mom before she died.

"How often do you come back home, Mason?" Joey asked.

"At least once a year for the holidays," I answered.

"Or his mama would kill him," Aunt Savannah said.

Everyone laughed. It was true. When I moved across country, my mother made me swear that as long as she was alive I would come back for the holidays. Guilt trips. The weapon of choice by mothers everywhere.

"Well, I've got to tell you, Joey ..." Katie began.

I shot her a look. I had no idea where the hell this would go.

"Mason's mentioned you before," she said, smiling and winking at me.

"Oh, really?" Joey said, cocking an eyebrow.

"Yeah, about this handsome guy he went all gaga for when he lived with his aunt. And I must say, coming from a big old lesbian here, you are just as cute as Mason said you were."

Joey blushed.

"Well, thanks to both of you then," Joey said.

Embarrassed, I kicked Katie under the table, but she just grinned.

"Wait! Where's all of your luggage?" Savannah asked Joey, as all of us headed back in the direction of Savannah's home in the heart of the Quarter.

"I dropped them off at the hotel on the way here," Joey answered.

Savannah stopped in the middle of the street and put her hands on her hips. Behind her in a bar, we heard a drunk college aged girl sing a bad karaoke version of "It's Raining Men."

"Hotel!" Savannah exclaimed. "Well, go pick them up! I haven't seen you in how many years? You're staying with me!"

"Oh, I can't impose, so ..." Joey began to say.

"Impose, my D cup tits!" Savannah said. "You're staying in the extra bedroom. Not up for debate."

She threw her hands up in the air.

Katie elbowed me and smiled.

"Uh, well, okay, if you're sure," Joey said.

"Of course I'm sure," Savannah said. "Now let's go pick those bags up."

She started to walk ahead and took Katie's arm on one side and Clayton on the other.

"Don't you just love the Quarter at night," Savannah said wistfully.

A horse drawn carriage with a young couple went by us, and I could hear the driver tell them, "In that house, Tennessee Williams wrote A Streetcar Named Desire."

I found Joey and I slowed our steps until it was just the two of us walking a good six feet behind the rest of the group.

"Looks like we're going to be spending a lot of time together over the next few days," I said to him.

"Yeah. It'll be nice to catch up after all of this time," Joey said.

In the background, I could hear Savannah telling Katie and Clayton a story about when Johnny Depp attended one of her shows.

"Joey, I know it's been a lot of years," I started to say to him in a half-whisper. "I just wanted to say I'm sorry for …"

I felt Joey's hand on my back.

"No need, Mason. Like you said, it's been a lot of years. Any misunderstandings are ancient history. Anyway, we were just kids back then."

It felt like my apology lifted a great weight off my chest after so many years.

"You're right, aren't you? We were just babies back then."

"But thought we were all grown," Joey said, smiling.

"Geez, I can't believe it's been twelve years. It doesn't seem like that long to me. You?"

"Not really. No."

He smiled at me again, and inside, after all of these years, my heart melted.

CHAPTER 8

"Mason! Your stupid phone won't stop ringing!" I heard Katie yell from the other room in Savannah's guesthouse.

I glanced at the clock in my bedroom and saw that it was only 7:30 AM. I wondered who the hell would be calling repeatedly at this time of the morning.

"Mason!" Katie screamed.

"I'm coming!" I yelled back.

I stumbled out of bed wearing my boxers and my San Francisco Pride 2003 T-shirt and made my way to the other room.

"Stupid phone," Katie grumbled, placing her pillow over her head.

"Sorry," I said. "I don't know who the hell it could be."

I went over to the kitchenette counter where my phone sat. It started to ring again. The screen read "Four Missed Calls". I checked out the phone and saw Colin's name number flashing. It was only 5:30 in San Francisco.

"It's Colin!" I said to Katie. "What should I do?"

She lifted the pillow from her head and looked at me with piercing eyes.

"Answer that phone and I kill you," she said.

Part of me badly wanted to answer. Maybe there was some sort of emergency? Hell, no. That wasn't it. I wanted to answer because a part of me still cared.

"Maybe it's an emergency," I said.

The phone continued to ring.

"The only emergency is that he wants to fuck with your head," she said.

I took a deep breath and turned off the phone.

"There," I said.

"Good. Now can I go back to sleep?" Katie pleaded.

"Yeah, I think I'm up now. I'm going to go to Savannah's kitchen to see if there's any coffee."

Katie mumbled an incoherent response and turned back over.

I walked outside the guesthouse into the courtyard to find that the sun was already shining brightly. I could hear a garbage truck rumble by outside the walls surrounding Savannah's house. The birds were already happily chirping. Damn birds, I thought, irritated at being woken up so early.

I walked up the stairs to Savannah's kitchen, lifted the cactus that I knew she stored the spare key under, and let myself inside.

Immediately, I made my way over to the large container of Community Coffee, dark roast with chicory.

"Hey there!" I heard Joey say behind me.

I turned around to find him standing in the kitchen doorway wearing running shorts and a white tank top.

"Oh, hi," I said.

I glanced down at my ratty T-shirt and Fruit of the Loom white boxers. Then I remembered that my hair probably stood straight up on end as it usually did in the mornings. And there was Joey in a running outfit looking sweaty and sexy.

"Looking for the coffeemaker?" he asked.

"Huh?"

He motioned to the coffee container I held in my hand.

"Oh, uh, yeah," I said.

He pointed to the other counter to Savannah's coffeemaker.

"I thought you'd probably still be in bed since you're on West Coast time," he said.

"Me, too," I said. "But I'm up. Coffee?"

"Sure," Joey said, and sat at the dinette table. "I guess Savannah and Clayton are still asleep."

"Yeah, I think so," I said, pouring water into the coffeepot. "I'm impressed. You've already been out running?"

"I took a run along the river. I usually do at least three miles in the morning back in New York."

The most exercise I got in the mornings was walking to the bathroom to take a piss.

I sat down at the table while the coffee percolated. I tried to smooth down my hair with my hand.

Another moment of awkward silence.

"So ..." Joey and I said simultaneously.

We both laughed.

"It's wild seeing you after so long," I said.

"Yeah, you, too. It surprised me when Savannah tracked me down and told me she wanted me at the wedding."

"She missed you a lot when you left," I said.

"I missed her and New Orleans, too. But it was time for me to see more of the world."

"I went to Shreveport looking for you after you left," I told him.

"Yeah, I know," he said. "My aunt mentioned it to me about a year later. I don't know why she didn't tell me sooner. I think she wanted me to go to New York to keep an eye on my cousin. It pissed me off she didn't say anything before. And by the time she mentioned it, I figured so much time had gone by. When did you go to San Fran?"

"Not long after finishing school," I said. "Again, I'm sorry."

"And again, there's no need to apologize. We were just teenagers back then." He paused. "I think the coffee's ready."

I got up, poured us both a cup, and took out the sugar and half and half.

"Thanks," Joey said, taking the cup of piping hot java out of my hands.

I sat back down.

"What do you plan to do in the time we have before the wedding?" I asked.

"Since I haven't been here in so long, I want to visit some of the old haunts and neighborhoods. Plus, I want to have a few po-boys!"

I took a deep breath and asked ...

"Before everyone else gets moving, I thought about taking the trolley through the Garden District to snap some pictures. Want to come along?"

"Sure. That'd be great," Joey answered, before looking down at his sweaty clothes that I thought he looked hot wearing. "I should probably take a quick shower though."

"Yeah, me, too. Want to meet in the courtyard in fifteen minutes?"

"Sounds great!" Joey said.

I took a speedy shower and tried to make myself as presentable as possible in fifteen minutes. I know it may sound silly since he had just seen me a few minutes before. Inside, I felt all giddy and nervous like a teenager going on a first date. I told myself to calm down. Joey and I were nothing more than two old friends catching up.

After meeting back up, we walked a few blocks down to catch the streetcar on St. Charles Avenue. The streetcar, full of morning commuters, made its way from the Garden District to the CBD, or Central Business District.

Both us stayed pretty quiet, sort of just taking in the scenery of the city we both once called home.

While riding, I remembered the first day Joey and I hung out together all of those years before. At the time, I felt so embarrassed because I thought Aunt Savannah had forced him to spend the day with me, but later that day, I already sensed we had a connection.

"Your aunt asked if I would just spend some time showing you around today."

I felt embarrassed that this poor guy had been roped into entertaining me for the day. My aunt was his boss, so I knew he couldn't say no. What was she up to with all of this?

Joey led me to a couple of art galleries on Royal, where Savannah had ordered some new artwork for the theater and he had to drop off the checks for payment. They told us the paintings would be delivered to the theater later that day.

While Joey waited for a receipt, I browsed around in one of the art galleries. I had never been to a gallery or even a real museum. I didn't think the small museum that was dedicated to the Andrews family at the library back home counted. I was fascinated by some of the paintings. The detail was amazing, from the colors to all of the little nuances that each artist had added. I was also fascinated by the prices! Some of the paintings and sculptures ran in the thousands. I wondered who had that kind of money just to spend on a painting. Then I wondered how much Savannah had paid, because I figured that nothing there was cheap.

"Ready to go?" Joey asked. He folded the receipt and put it in his backpack.

"Where to now?"

"I'll give you the grand tour," he said smiling.

First, we went to Jackson Square, where I remembered seeing that huge, old church, the St. Louis Cathedral, during my last visit. That day, the areas outside the square, which included a small park in front of the church, were alive with activity. Mimes, clowns trying to sell balloon animals, artists painting quick portraits of tourists, and tarot card readers were everywhere. The tarot card readers who had set up shop with just a TV tray and a couple of crates were the funniest, I thought. Joey told me that if I wanted my cards read, he could take me to a "real" reader who worked out of one of the voodoo shops in the Quarter.

We then went to a bakery called La Madeleine, where Joey bought us the best pastry I had ever eaten. It was topped with creamy icing and stuffed with fresh blueberries, and we ate them sitting on benches in the Square.

"Any place in particular you would like to go?" Joey asked.

I was watching the parade of people go by. The whole place felt alive with energy, and I found myself so happy that I had gotten out of Andrews Springs. Back home, the most excitement you could hope for was a new movie at the show. But in New Orleans, and in the French Quarter, the energy of the place suggested that there would be boundless things for me to do during my trip.

"I don't think I even know where to begin," I said.

"I know where we can start," Joey said.

He grabbed my hand and pulled me up. I was a little taken aback by this physical gesture, but I just smiled and followed him down Decatur Street.

Along the way, he really began to open up as he got more comfortable around me. He told me he was born and raised in New Orleans. Of course, I already knew that because of what my aunt had told me, but I didn't tell him that. He said he enjoyed painting, and one day he hoped to save up enough money to go to art school. Turns out he had been to the galleries we had been to earlier that morning quite a few times, and he also liked going to the local museums. He felt fascinated by everything an artist could convey with simple paint and a canvas.

We found ourselves along the Mississippi River, on what he called the Moon-walk. We strolled along as the ships and tourist steamboats went by. He told me the current in the river was so strong that if you fell in the muddy, brown water, you might as well "kiss your ass goodbye."

Tourists walked along with us. Some paused briefly to take pictures of the boats. A Japanese couple stopped us and asked Joey if he would take their picture. He did, and the young couple seemed so much in love standing next to a lamppost with the river in the background. I wondered if I would ever experience the love and contentment that was in their eyes when they looked at each other.

We continued on past the Aquarium, which Joey said I had to visit before I left because they had some really cool albino alligators that just had to be seen. We then went to the Riverwalk mall, which included both national chain stores and local ones selling things I had never seen before ...

Chicken foot keychains? Baby alligator heads? Yuck!

I noticed Joey looking into the windows of some of the stores with eyes of wonderment himself. I sensed that he had never had much money, and that he probably had never actually shopped at the Riverwalk. Yet he seemed to know every single shop there, and what they sold.

After we left the mall, we walked a few blocks down Canal Street along stores that sold a lot of what Joey called "tourist crap": cheap plastic Mardi Gras beads, Mardi Gras masks, those weird little snow globes (snow in New Orleans?), and the like.

Joey, who had been so shy, had almost become a motormouth. He had a story for every building and every street corner. My fears that Savannah had dragged him into showing me around town waned, as he really seemed to be enjoying himself.

When we turned off Canal onto a street called Burgundy, he told me he lived in a small apartment just a few blocks up. He said the only way he could afford it was that my aunt paid part of the rent each month. He actually got a little teary-eyed when he mentioned it.

"My mom died a little over a year ago," he said.

"I'm sorry," I said. I made sure to act a little surprised. I wouldn't want him to think that Savannah had told me all of his business.

"She started working for your aunt right after she bought the theater. I guess I was born a little over a year after that," he said. We continued walking along what was mainly a residential area. "Ever since my mom died, I guess, Miss Savannah has kinda been keeping an eye out for me. I don't know what I would do without her."

As the streetcar made its way through the Garden District, we watched early morning joggers run along the street near the campuses of both Tulane and Loyola.

I looked down at the camera in my lap. I wondered if it had been such a good idea to ask Joey to come along. I didn't know how much work I would get done in his presence. He made me so nervous, but in a good way.

We got off the trolley at Carrollton, and started walking along the sidewalks of the Garden District. Historic homes and quaint little shops selling antiques lined both sides of the street. I immediately took pictures of any sights that struck me.

"It's amazing that you became a photographer. I'm very proud of you," Joey said. "Savannah told me about your book of photography on Chinatown. Very impressive."

"Thanks," I replied. "Growing up, I never even thought about it. Now, it's my passion," I replied. "Want to sit for a moment?" I asked, motioning towards a bench.

"Sure."

We sat down and deeply inhaled the fresh morning air. I had always been a morning person. To me, the morning environment with its sense of a new beginning always energized me.

I turned and looked at Joey, the morning light made his steel gray eyes sparkle all the more.

"I'm not surprised you became a social worker," I said. "You were always so compassionate. Even when you had a lot of reasons not to be."

"It's not always the world's easiest job, believe me. But it makes me feel good to know I'm making a difference," Joey said.

"And, so … is there … a significant other in your life?" I asked.

"There … was," he answered.

"Ah, yeah, me, too," I said.

"Yeah, I know. I wondered because Savannah had said you were bringing your boyfriend with you."

I fiddled with my lens cap. I really didn't want to tell Joey that Billy had been part of the reason for the relationship's end.

"You don't have to tell me anything about it if you don't want to," Joey said. "It's okay."

He gave me a reassuring smile, and maybe it had been only in my mind, but I could swear he rubbed his leg against mine-on purpose.

"It's just all a little fresh for me," I said. "Kinda hard to deal with."

Joey nodded.

"I understand. I lived with my ex, Juan, for almost three years. Everything went great at first. Then, I don't know, one day we just didn't seem to have anything to talk about any more. I think part of it had to do with our age. We were so young when we got together."

I sighed.

"Yeah, it's amazing how much you learn about yourself and the world in your twenties. I guess though … this just isn't where I thought I'd end up at this point in life."

"Yeah, but who's to say it's not where you're exactly supposed to be at this point. I'm not sure I believe in predestination, but sometimes I think we have to go through certain experiences in life to learn certain lessons," Joey said, smiling.

I swear that smile still warmed my heart after all of these years.

My stomach rumbled from hunger, and we both laughed.

"I think someone needs lunch," Joey said.

"Yeah, maybe that's a good idea."

We stood up and began to walk to the streetcar stop.

"Joey?"

"Yeah?"

"I'm really glad you came for the wedding. I can't tell you how great it is to see you."

"Me, too," he said, giving me a tight hug.

We walked into Savannah's courtyard to find her and Clayton sitting at a table eating sandwiches and drinking Savannah's extra sweet Southern iced tea.

"Just in time for lunch," Clayton said.

"Thank God. I'm starved," I said, making my way over to the table.

Savannah got up and pulled out two chairs for me and Joey.

"Have a seat, babies. I'll be right back with your lunch," she said.

"You don't have to go to any …" Joey began.

"Shhhhh," Savannah said. "Sit down and get ready to eat."

"Thanks, Aunt Savannah," I said as Joey and I both sat down.

Before she left for the kitchen, Savannah looked at Joey and me and beamed.

"Look at that, Clayton. Both of my boys are home again," she said, before heading into the kitchen.

"As you can tell, she's very happy the two of you are here, and I love to see my girl happy," Clayton said. "I'm so pleased that both of you are going to be here for the wedding."

"Thanks," Joey said. "That means a lot to hear. I'm just sorry I didn't get to meet you earlier."

"Me, too," I said.

"The important thing is that you're both here now," Clayton said.

Savannah walked back out carrying two huge glasses of iced tea for Joey and me.

"Are all ya'll talkin' about me?" Savannah asked.

"Yes, but only the good stuff," I replied.

"I should hope so!" Savannah said. "My wedding is coming up!"

CHAPTER 9

"That is so disgusting," Katie said, crinkling her nose.

We sat on barstools as a male stripper, just a couple of feet from us, spun his penis around and around like a helicopter blade to blasting dance music at one of my favorite old haunts in the Quarter, The Prowler.

"Speak for yourself, sister," I said, captivated by the tall, dark, and muscled stripper.

"Boys!" Katie said, rolling her eyes. "I just don't get the penis thing."

I took a slug of my rum and Coke.

"That's why you're a lesbian," I said, laughing.

"True."

It felt so wild being out with Katie in New Orleans, drinking and laughing, for the first time together.

"The rest of your family will be here soon," Katie said.

"Yeah, I know," I said, with a hint of dread.

"Why are you so nervous about telling them that you and Colin are finished?"

My attention turned from the stripper down to my drink while I contemplated Katie's question.

"I guess I felt like I spent so much time convincing them I could have a happy life as a gay man, and now this …"

"Oh, so, straight people never break up or get divorced?"

"I know it sounds stupid."

Katie put her arm around me and began swaying to the music.

"No, it's not stupid. But they'll understand."

"And speaking of family …"

Katie's sigh was so loud I could hear it over the dance music.

"I'll call them," she replied.

"When? We're not here for that long," I reminded her.

"Yeah, yeah, yeah," Katie mumbled.

A young lipstick lesbian wearing a leather miniskirt walked by and made *very* direct eye contact with Katie.

"Damn! Hot!" Katie said to me.

Lipstick Lesbian walked across the bar, but her stare stayed fixed on Katie.

"Obviously, she wants to talk to you," I said. "Go!"

I gave her a soft push on the back.

"I came here to hang out with you. I'm not going to leave you by yourself," Katie said.

I could see the red hot desire in her eyes though.

"Well, hey there!" we heard a voice call out from behind us.

We turned around and found Joey, looking as lickable as ever in a tight gray tank top and jeans that managed to show off every attribute of his exquisite manhood without going too far.

"Hi!" I said. I leaned into Katie. "See, I won't be alone."

Katie smiled.

"I'll be back," she said before dashing off to talk to Lipstick Lesbian.

Joey sat next to me and ordered a beer.

"Looks like Katie found a new friend," he said, smiling.

"Sure looks that way."

The stripper danced by on top of the bar and smiled at Joey.

Joey cracked up and laughed.

"I forgot just how crazy this town can be. It makes New York look like a nursery school."

The dancer winked at him, and then made his way down the bar where some young college-aged kids were waving dollar bills.

"I think he likes you," I said.

"He's something else," is all Joey said.

"Nowhere near as handsome as you," I said.

Alcohol and speaking before you think always equaled a bad combination.

Joey grinned.

"Thanks, but I don't know about that," he said.

What the hell …

"I do," I said.

Couple of moments of weird silence.

"I hoped I'd run into you," he said.

"Really?"

"After I did some shopping, I took a wild guess at to where you may be."

"Amazing how fast you can fall back into old habits. How many nights did we hang out at The Prowler as kids?"

"God only know," Joey said. "And the most amazing part is that we lived to tell the story."

I giggled.

"True, but I guess we have some stories to share in the old gay folks home."

"That's a good way to look at it," Joey said, before ordering another beer from the bartender.

We watched a montage of scenes from "Mommie Dearest" that played on the large video screens. Edited to play over and over, Faye Dunaway screamed, "No more! No more! No more! No more! Wire hangers! Ever! Ever! Ever!"

People throughout the bar rolled with laughter.

I leaned in closer to Joey to be heard.

"There's something I didn't tell you about Colin … about the break-up."

"You don't have to tell me anything you don't want to. It's none of my business," Joey said.

The classic "It's Raining Men" began to blare in the background.

"I know. You might find it a little funny."

"Funny?"

"The reason I left Colin. You remember, my old friend, Billy?"

Joey chuckled.

"How could I forget?"

"I walked in on him fucking my boyfriend," I said, staring into my cocktail.

"Whoa," Joey said, taken aback. "I'm sorry. I don't know what to say."

"I didn't either when I walked into the apartment. Kinda ironic, huh?" I said.

"How do you mean?"

"It's like I'll never learn when it comes to him."

"Have you now?" Joey asked, cocking an eyebrow.

"Yeah, big time. I feel like such an idiot. And it's not like Billy was force feeding Colin his cock."

I felt myself start to tear up … but I would *not* allow myself to start crying in The Prowler of all places.

"I felt so humiliated. Two people I trusted. So stupid of me."

I downed the rest of my drink.

"Stop being so hard on yourself. It's both Colin and Billy's loss, you know? You're a good guy, Mason. You try and see the good in everyone."

"That can get you in trouble sometimes," I said.

Across the bar, Katie waved at me and pointed outside the door to let me know she was leaving with Lipstick Lesbian.

I held up my empty drink glass to her and smiled.

"Looks like someone scored big," Joey said. "Wondered where they're headed?"

"I doubt it's the St. Louis Cathedral," I replied.

"Not unless your friend, Katie, is *real* kinky," Joey said.

I felt my cell phone vibrate in my pocket. Not Colin, not now, I thought.

I took the phone out and saw Savannah's number flashing.

"It's Aunt Savannah," I said, turning around and walking out one of The Prowler's entrances that exited onto St. Anne Street.

Joey followed me, carrying his beer in one of New Orleans's famous "go cups." You could leave a bar with your cocktail and take it outside as long as it was in a plastic cup. You gotta love that.

I flipped open the phone with one hand and covered my other ear to try and hear over the thump-a-thump of the dance music that spilled out onto the street.

"Hey, Auntie," I said. "What's up?"

The sound on the other end was muffled at first, but then I heard, "Mason, this is Clayton. I'm with your aunt at the hospital."

"Hospital!" I exclaimed.

Joey, his eyes full of worry, set his drink on the ground.

"Okay, I'll be there in a sec," I said and then hung up.

"Shit, you're white as a sheet! What's wrong?" Joey asked.

"It's Savannah," I said. "She's in the hospital. We've got to go."

"I'll get a cab," Joey said, frantically running off.

I stood there frozen, seemingly unable to move. Partiers poured out the bar and walked around me, talking and laughing, making their way to the next party destination.

I didn't know exactly what had happened, but Clayton sounded worried. Very worried.

CHAPTER 10

A weary Clayton stood up from the waiting room chair as Joey and I walked in the emergency hospital waiting room.

"How is she?" I asked, my voice cracking.

"She's fine," Clayton said. "The nurse is with her now."

"What happened?" Joey asked.

"We were just home having dinner, and she started having some pains in her chest," Clayton said.

"Oh, Jesus," I said and impulsively grabbed Joey's arm.

"At first she tried to play it off … like nothing was wrong," Clayton said, shaking his head. His eyes were bloodshot and his skin looked unusually pale.

"Heart attack?" I asked.

My mind flashed back to when my father had had a heart attack when I was living with Aunt Savannah. I had rushed right home, and I had never felt so scared. Part of me still felt guilty for being in San Francisco when he later passed away.

"At first I was scared it was one," Clayton said.

He took a handkerchief out of his pocket and wiped his brow.

"What do they think now?" Joey asked.

"The doctor thinks it just may be stress from planning all the wedding stuff," Clayton said. He shook his head. "I tried to talk her into hiring a wedding planner, but she insisted she wanted to do everything herself. I guess …"

Clayton's eyes began to well up, and I placed a hand on his shoulder.

"It's not your fault, Clayton. She's just all wound up with all of the planning. That's all. I know how special she wants the wedding day to be."

Clayton couldn't hold back anymore, as tears began to drift down his cheeks.

"The only thing that matters to me is having the two of us there and the people we love. Nothing else matters," he said.

"I know," I said, squeezing his shoulder.

A young, perky female nurse walked out into the hall and Clayton jumped to attention.

"How is she?" he asked.

"She's fine, baby," the nurse said, reassuringly. "She's even putting on a little make-up right now. Says she has to freshen her face."

All three of us chuckled, and some of the tension finally broke.

"Can we see her?" I asked.

"Sure. Just for a few minutes though. She needs her rest."

"Of course," I said.

We walked in to find Savannah, sure enough, applying powder while staring into a compact. She looked up at all of us and sighed.

"Well, good Lord, look at those faces. I'm fine. Everybody can perk up."

Both Joey and I ran over to her and placed kisses on her cheeks.

"Jesus Christ," I said. "Are you trying to scare the shit out of us or what?"

"Clayton, honey, can you dig the lipstick out of my purse?" she asked, pointing to her purse next to the bed.

Clayton dutifully began to dig through the mobile make-up counter Savannah referred to as her purse.

"How are you feeling?" Joey asked.

I sat on the bed next to her and started crying.

"Ah, Little Bit," she said, "Don't cry. I just got a little stressed out about the caterers, the cake, the band. I just need to, as you young people say 'chill out' a bit."

I wiped my tears with the back of my hand.

"Yes, chilling out would be a good idea," Clayton said, handing Savannah a tube of lipstick. I wondered how he knew which one to give her out of the fifteen or so she always carried.

"Doctor wants me to stay here for the night and get some good rest," she said, applying her lipstick with one hand and fluffing her hair with the other. "You know me. I can't even rest without making it all dramatic."

"Yes, well, a little less drama would be greatly appreciated," I said.

She reached over and patted my knee.

"Don't worry, Little Bit. I promise to be drama free all the way through the vows. Now, at the reception, I can't promise."

I laughed.

"You're so damn crazy," I said.

"And that's what ya'll love about me. Ain't that right, Clayton?" she said.

Clayton walked over and grabbed her hand. "More than you know, Blondie."

"I love you," Joey said, leaning down and accidentally pressing down Savannah's meticulously teased hair.

"I love you, too, baby," she said, holding him tight. "But be careful with the hair. It's tomorrow hair, you know."

I looked over at Clayton, who stared at my aunt with a look of such unconditional love and devotion. I felt happy that she finally found a wonderful man to treat her the way that she deserved.

"Well, let the lovebirds have some time before Auntie needs to get rest," I said.

"See you in the morning?" Joey said.

"As soon as Clayton can spring me from this joint," Savannah said, smiling at her fiancé.

Joey and I gave her one last hug, and walked out back into the waiting room.

Katie came running toward me, looking disheveled with her pink hair sticking out in all directions. On the way to the hospital, I called her on her cell and told her we would be at the hospital.

She threw her arms around me.

"I'm so sorry, Mason! How's your aunt?"

"She's fine," I assured her.

"Thank God! I felt so bad when I got your voicemail. I had been in the middle of … well …"

"Katie, it's okay. Really," I said. "Everything's fine."

Katie took a deep breath and sighed.

"Are you sure?" she asked.

"Yes, why don't you go back and get some sleep. It's late. I think I'm going to hang out here a bit longer."

Katie looked a bit hesitant.

"Don't worry. I'll keep him company," Joey said.

"Promise me that you'll call me if you need me," she said.

"Promise."

After Katie left, I leaned my tired head on Joey's shoulder, and he put his arms around me and held me tight.

"I was so scared," I whispered in his ear.

"I know," he said.

"You don't have to hang out here, you know?" I said.

"Mason, there's no place I'd rather be right now. Savannah's like my family, too."

"I know."

"How about we go get a horrible cup of vending machine coffee?" he asked.

"Sounds great," I said.

We took our cups of coffee and sat on a bench outside the emergency room entrance getting some fresh air, or as fresh as you could get in New Orleans.

After a few moments of silence, Joey asked, "Do you ever miss New Orleans?"

"Yeah, sometimes. The food, the people, and of course, my family. I miss them a lot sometimes. But I don't regret going to San Francisco. It's a great city, and I've learned so much by being there … different cultures, politics."

"Yeah, same thing with me in New York," Joey said.

"And you?" I asked. "Think you'll ever come back to the Big Easy?"

"I guess I've learned at this point in life never to say never about anything."

He looked down into his cup of coffee and then looked back up at me.

"Tastes like crap, huh?" I said.

He smiled.

"Majorly."

I looked down at my watch.

"Maybe we should head back and get some sleep. I'm sure Clayton will stay here," I said.

"Sure, let's go tell him, and I'll call us a cab."

Clayton stood in the hallway outside Savannah's room. He leaned against the wall and looked like he could just slide down the wall at any second and fall on the floor. He looked beyond exhausted.

"Clayton, Joey and I …"

"She's gone," he mumbled.

"What?" Joey said.

"Clayton," I said, touching his arm. "What are you talking about?"

"Just a few minutes ago," he started to sob. "She had a heart attack, and they tried to revive her and …"

"No," I muttered, stepping back a couple of feet. "Savannah!"

I started to bolt through the door into her room. Joey grabbed my arm.

"Mason, wait!" he pleaded.

I pulled away, and went into the room. The nurse, who before looked so bubbly, gave me a look of condolence.

"God, no!" Joey said.

I felt him embrace me from behind and bury his face into my neck. I stood there motionless. My eyes on my aunt. She looked so peaceful and at rest. Her make-up-perfect.

CHAPTER 11

The next few days went by in a blur, and I don't seem to recall many details. I guess because I felt so dazed, or I was in denial-or maybe both.

I met my family outside Savannah's house when they arrived. My mother had been the first one of out the car, followed by my sister, Cherie, brother-in-law, Houston, and finally my niece, Lily.

Mother said a quick hello and immediately began unloading luggage out of the trunk of the car. She had never been one to wear her emotions on her sleeve, but I knew her well enough to know that that did not mean she was not suffering inside.

I walked over, made her stop unloading suitcases, and gave her a big hug.

"I'm so sorry," I whispered in her ear.

For a second, I felt her embrace around me tighten, and then she pulled away.

"Help us carry some of this in," she said, motioning towards the luggage.

"I will," I said, my voice cracking.

Cherie ran up to me and gave me a big hug.

"Hey, little brother," she said. Her eyes began to well with tears. "This isn't how this trip was supposed to happen."

I wiped a tear from her face.

"I know," I said softly.

Houston, always a man of few words, shook my hand and began to haul the luggage inside.

I turned to my niece. She had grown what seemed like three inches since I saw her the past Christmas. She was quickly becoming a young woman, one as beautiful as her mother had been at the same age.

I tried to put on my best brave face as I waved her to come over to me.

"Uncle Mason," she said, hugging me tightly.

"My Lily girl, you've grown so much since I last saw you," I said.

I felt my heart tugging over the fact that I had been missing so much of her growing up. Lily had been an "accident" on my sister and Houston's part, but she turned out to be the best thing that ever happened to the family. Her sense of humor reminded me of Savannah's, and she always had the ability to unite my family in the middle of any conflict.

I took her hand, looked at my mom and Cherie, and said, "Let's go on in. Clayton's waiting to see everyone."

Despite being devastated, Clayton made all of the arrangements with the help of Joey. If you watched the television, it looked like the whole city was in mourning. On the news, in the papers, on the streets everyone talked about my aunt's death. She had managed to become such a New Orleans icon that everyone loved her.

At the funeral, many of the New Orleans elite were in attendance-the Connicks, the Nevilles, and many city officials.

My niece, Lily, looked distraught. Savannah had become the same magical aunt to Lily as she had done with me. Lily looked forward to all of Savannah's visits, and she always brought Lily a shiny new toy, or as she got older new clothes from the finest boutiques in New Orleans. She enjoyed listening to all of Savannah's fascinating stories about living in the Quarter, just as I had.

I didn't know if I would make it through as they lowered Savannah's coffin into the ground. Joey reached out for my hand and squeezed it. I looked over and he was crying as hard as me.

My aunt had always been my rock, the person I knew I could always count on, the person who understood me-for me-from the beginning. She had been the first one in the family I came out to, or rather she made me come out to her, bless her heart.

We drove off down the streets crowded with cars and people. We went past the gay bars I had seen during my last visit. I couldn't help but look inside as we drove.

"Saw you looking," Savannah giggled.

I quickly turned away, ashamed.

"Oh, it's okay," she quickly said. "I thought you might end up wanting to spend some time in that part of the Quarter."

I felt myself blush.

"Uh …" I started to say.

"It's completely okay, and I won't report anything back to Andrew Springs. Promise," she said. She reached over and patted my knee.

I took a deep breath.

"How did you know?" I finally said.

"Sweetie, I've known lots of different people over the years. It wasn't hard for me to figure out which side your bread was buttered on. That was one of the reasons you wanted to spend some time here in the city, right?"

Caught.

I smiled weakly.

"Kinda," I answered.

"I figured as much. That's why I pressed your mother so much to let you come." I had just come out to my aunt, and I had totally not been expecting to do so.

After the funeral, I sat out on Savannah's balcony trying to rest in some silence before the crowds of expected mourners were expected to arrive.

Katie walked out and sat beside me.

"Hanging in there?" she asked.

"As best I can," I said.

She laid her head on my shoulder.

"You'll be proud of me," she said.

"Why?

"With everything that's happened, it got me thinking. So, I called my parents. They're on their way to New Orleans right now to see me before I leave."

I put my arm around me.

"I'm glad to hear it," I said.

"Me, too. If you can believe it, I'm actually looking forward to seeing them."

"I can believe it," I replied.

She squeezed me knee.

"I'm going to go help Joey set out some food," she said.

"Need my help?" I asked.

"Nope, you just rest," she answered.

We both looked over and saw Lily walk out onto the balcony.

"Besides," Katie said, "I think you have company."

Katie got up and went back inside.

Lily wore the dress Savannah had given her the previous summer. She looked a little scared to approach me. I guess unsure about my state of mind and if I wanted to be alone.

I smiled and motioned her over.

"Come on over, Lily girl," I said.

She sat down next to me, and I put my arm around her.

"How are you doing?" I asked.

She shrugged her shoulders.

I nodded my head.

"I know. I feel the same way," I said.

"It's just so sad. Her wedding was supposed to be today."

"Yeah, it's hard to believe," I said, reaching over and smoothing down her chestnut colored hair, just as Savannah would do with me.

"Today was supposed to be the wedding. We were supposed to have a party right now. Not this."

"Things don't always go as planned," I said.

Those were the only words of wisdom I could come up with?

Lily looked up at me and asked, "Why would God do this?"

"Who knows why a lot of things happen?" I said. "What I do know is that Aunt Savannah loved you a lot."

"I know. It just … it all sucks," she said.

I thought my thirteen-year-old niece pretty much summed up everything quite well in that one sentence.

She ran her fingers through her hair.

"Mom was going to braid my hair for me today, but she's helping Grandma set up the food."

"Sit on the floor," I said. "I'll do it for you."

"You can braid hair?" she said.

"Lily girl, what's the point in having a gay uncle if I can't at least braid your hair for you? And I'd probably do a better job than your mom."

Lily laughed.

What seemed like a never-ending wave of guests came through Savannah's door. Each person made an attempt to express their condolences to her whole family. All of Savannah's performers from the theater came dressed up in full drag. I'm sure Savannah would not have expected or wanted it any other way.

Miss Althea gave me a giant bear hug. I had no idea how strong she was underneath all the wig, dresses, and make-up.

"Baby, your auntie was the best," Miss Althea said. "She practically took this lost little boy/girl off the streets of the Quarters, and turned her into Miss Althea-somebody in this town. I'll never forget what she's done for me."

"She loved you a lot, Miss Althea. You were her star," I said.

Miss Althea nodded.

"I sho' was, wasn't I?" she said. "Course, without her directions, I would've been nowhere. Probably hanging out with some of dem rough trades across the river."

She wiped a tear from her eye with a bright red handkerchief.

"What are we supposed to do without her? What about the cabaret?"

The theater, of course, had remained dark since Savannah's death. I hadn't even stopped to think about all of the people she employed. I remembered she said that if she sold the place, she would give everyone a huge severance. Now what would happen to them all? In a town like New Orleans, there weren't exactly a lot of job openings for full-time drag queens.

"I don't know," I said. "I guess everything will be figured out one thing at a time."

"Well, if you need anything, you let me know," Miss Althea said, giving me another hug.

"Thanks, Miss Althea."

She looked over at Joey talking to some of the other drag queens in attendance.

"Seems just like yesterday the two of yous were just young chickens, straight out of the coop, all googly eyes over each other."

She sighed.

"It all goes so fast," she said.

"Back then I couldn't wait to be older," I said. "Now … I wish things could slow down."

Althea winked at me.

"What about you and that boy? Any chance the two of you might make your ways back to each other after all these years?"

"I don't know. That was a really long time ago."

"Look," Miss Althea said, "If Miss Althea can finally find herself a *huzzband*, anybody can do it."

I smiled and glanced over at Miss Althea's *"huzzband"*, Paul, a man probably in his early sixties with salt and pepper hair, a slight belly pooch, and a kind face. He piled a paper plate high with food.

"I know he ain't much to look at," Miss Althea said.

I playfully slapped her arm.

"Miss Althea!" I exclaimed.

"Well, honey, it's the truth! But he sure does treat me well. Like a true queen!" she said. "And at this age, baby, that means everything to me."

"I know how hard it is to find a good man," I said.

Miss Althea cocked an eyebrow.

"Not if you keep your eyes open," she said, while looking in Joey's direction. "I better go keep an eye on my *huzzband* and all that fried food."

She took off, and before I could move, Katie stood at my side.

"I have a couple of people who want to meet you," she said.

She moved over and I immediately recognized her parents from a picture in her apartment. They looked like the perfect prim and proper Southern couple. Her distinguished looking dad wore a gray suit. You could easily picture him behind a church pulpit. Her mother wore a tasteful black pantsuit, understated jewelry, and as so many Southern women, perfect make-up.

"We've heard so much about you, Mason, from our Katie. I'm glad to meet you. Just wish it were under better circumstances."

Her father held out his hand.

"Likewise," he said. "I'm Sam Martin and this is my wife, Dee."

"It's nice to meet you both," I said, surprised at their sudden appearance.

"After Katie told us about your aunt," her mom began, "we wanted to stop by and pay our respects. She sounds like a wonderful lady from what Katie's been saying."

"Thank you," I said, still in amazement that Katie's parents actually stood before me.

Even though I couldn't imagine their reaction at finding their daughter's dildo in the couch, they looked like warm people.

"Thank you for bringing our daughter back home, at least for a visit," her father said, smiling. "It'd been way too long since we'd seen her."

Katie, *yes Katie*, actually beamed.

It is true that standing next to each other you would never group this three in the same family, but then, in their eyes you could see it was true.

Before Katie had to fly back, I told her to take her parents out to dinner and spend some quality time with them.

"Are you sure you'll be okay?" she asked.

"Of course, now go. I want you to visit with your mom and dad before you fly back."

She kissed me on the cheek.

"Careful," I joked. "People may get the wrong impression."

"Honey, I doubt that," she said. "Thanks, though, for making me do this. I'm glad you did."

Later, after most people had finally left, I walked into the kitchen to find my mother scrubbing out the sink. Cherie sat at the kitchen table drinking a cup of coffee.

I walked over and placed a kiss on my sister's forehead.

"Okay?" I asked.

"Yeah," she said. "I'm so proud of Lily. She's been so good through all of this, better than me."

"She's a great girl. You've done good."

"I'm still scared of the teenage years," Cherie said.

"Well, if I remember you at that age …"

Cherie waved her hand.

"Let's not talk about that. I don't even want to think about it."

I turned around and saw that Mother was *still* scrubbing the sink. I walked over to her and placed a hand on her back.

"Mother, the sink is already clean," I said, gently.

She looked at me with eyes full of sadness and frustration.

"Savannah liked a clean kitchen!" she said. "I'm not going to leave here without it being so."

Mother and Aunt Savannah had been polar opposites in every way imaginable. In fact, it was damn hard to picture them as sisters. My mother's more conservative demeanor was always in stark contrast to Aunt Savannah's wild antics. Still, I knew how much they loved and respected each other.

"I just think maybe you need to sit down for a moment. You've been going non-stop all day."

Mother took a deep breath.

"Mason, just let me handle this my way, okay," she said, her eyes welling up with tears.

"Okay, Mama," I said. I hadn't called her Mama in years,

I looked over at Cherie, who nodded her head, as if to say, "Let her be."

I headed back out to the balcony, where I found Clayton having a drink and watching a group of young school children being led down a Quarter street by a couple of nuns.

"The service was beautiful, Clayton," I said.

"I wanted the best for my, girl," he said.

"I know, and if you need any help before I fly out, with *anything*, please let me know."

"I think you may need to stay a few more days actually," he said.

"You need me to help with something?"

"It's not that. It's just … trust me, okay? Stay here for a few more days."

I had been planning on flying back to San Francisco the next day with Katie. I had to go back to work and begin to somehow trying to get my life back together without Colin or Savannah.

"Sure, if you say so," I said.

"Thanks," Clayton said.

That night, it was pointless trying to sleep. I tossed and turned. I couldn't believe that Savannah wasn't in the main house and that she was actually gone. She had been my rock and always my biggest supporter.

I finally decided just to get out of bed.

I took out my digital camera and began running through some of the shots I took of the city before Savannah died. I had to admit, the pictures were some of the best work I had done in awhile. The pictures had an energy and a vibrancy that none of my recent work in San Francisco displayed.

I glanced out the window and saw the morning's first light beaming. The clock read six forty-five.

I remembered my editor, Clarissa, left a message to speak with her, and I had left her a voicemail saying I had a family emergency and would call back as soon as I can.

From what I knew of Clarissa, I figured she had already been at the office for at least an hour, so I called.

"Yep, it's Clarissa," she answered.

"Hi, it's Mason."

I heard her exhale deeply-morning cigarette.

"How's your family, love?" she asked.

"Hanging in there," I answered, not really wanting to elaborate. "There's something I wanted to run by you."

"Go ahead," she said, and then I heard a slurp. Coffee.

"I feel like I've been banging my head against a wall coming up with a new idea for a book," I said.

"And?"

"I've been taking a lot of pictures since I've been in New Orleans, and I think they're pretty good. Actually, really good. What about a photography book with pictures from here? I'm not sure yet what theme I'd want to focus on, but it's the start of an idea."

Silence on the other end for a few second.

"I like it," she said. "A lot."

After my phone call to Clarissa, I felt more energized already, so I thought I would head out and snap a few more shots before the rest of the world got up.

I headed out to the courtyard to get some air, and I found Joey just getting off his phone.

"You're up already, too?" I asked.

"Yeah, can't sleep," he replied.

"Me, either," I said. "Making arrangements to go back to New York?" I asked.

"Actually, I'm delaying them for a few days."

"Yeah, me, too," I said.

"Clayton said he needed me to stay in town for a few more days," Joey said.

"He said the same thing to me."

Perplexed, we both looked at each other and wondered why Clayton needed us to stick around.

CHAPTER 12

Later that morning, I saw the rest my family off.

"Promise you'll email?" Lily asked.

"You bet, Lily girl," I said, while giving my niece one last bear hug.

"Everything's in the car," Houston said. "Everybody ready?"

Mother turned to me. Suddenly, she looked lost. He eyes darted all around.

"You're coming back for Christmas, right?" she said.

I embraced her.

"Of course, Mama," I said. I never called her momma anymore, but I had a feeling she needed to hear it right then at that moment.

"Call me soon," Cherie said, before getting into the car.

I watched their car slowly merge into the French Quarter traffic. Lily looked at me through the back window and waved. I waved back and tried to hold back more tears.

I stayed behind at Clayton's request. Before she left, he told my mother Savannah's lawyer would be contacting her in a few days regarding her final wishes.

Joey and I really didn't know what to think when Clayton invited us to lunch at Antoine's, one of the oldest restaurants in New Orleans.

Clayton greeted us at the door of the restaurant and then escorted us to a table where a tall handsome man in his forties stood up to greet us.

"Brewster Radcliffe," he said, as he shook our hands.

"Nice to meet you," Joey said.

I recognized the man from Aunt Savannah's funeral, but I had never been formally introduced to him.

We ordered and made some polite chitchat. Mr. Radcliffe offered his condolences to me.

"Thank you," I said. "But I think I speak for both myself and Joey that we're a little curious as to what this meeting has to do with."

Clayton cleared his throat.

"Maybe I should start," he said, looking over at Mr. Radcliffe, who nodded. "Mr. Radcliffe was Savannah's attorney. There's a specific reason I asked both you and Joey to stick around for a little bit."

"We thought so," Joey said.

"You have a big decision to make," Clayton said.

"Decision?" I asked, more confused than ever.

"After Savannah and I got engaged, we had our wills changed to reflect the upcoming changes in our lives," Clayton said.

"Makes sense," Joey said, looking at me out of the corner of his eye.

I know he wished as much as I did that everyone would get to the point.

"Savannah wanted to leave specific things to specific people. She left me the house in the Quarter," Clayton said. "A sum of money to your mother and sister. A trust fund for Lily. The will was written before she had begun to think about selling the business, and in it, she left the cabaret to you and Joey, equal parts, fifty-fifty."

"What? Are you serious?" I asked.

"She left us the whole business?" Joey asked.

"The theater and everything inside it to you boys," Clayton said. "Mason, she told me you were like the son she never had, as well as Joey. Joey, she also said the place would not have been the success it was if hadn't been for the hard work of your mother, who worked for her for years. She said it was only right that the both of you inherit the theater."

"I don't know what to say," I said, shocked.

The waiter delivered our entrees, but I couldn't even look at the food. I had not expected this at all. I looked over at a shocked Joey, and obviously, neither had he.

"This may sound silly, but what does this mean?" Joey asked.

"Your aunt was in the middle of negotiating the sale of the theater," Mr. Radcliffe said. "She was going to use the money from the sale to give her employees some compensation and then put the remainder in a fund for the two of you. But before the deal went through …"

"She died," I said.

"Mason. Joey. She loved both of you so much," Clayton said. "I'm sure she'd be happy with whatever decision the two of you make in regards to the theater."

"I can tell you how much the interested buyer was offering, and he's still interested," Mr. Radcliffe said.

He took out a pen and a small notepad and scribbled down a number and passed the paper across to me and Joey.

Both of our eyes widened when we saw it. Both of us had never been offered anything with so many zeros in the number.

"Oh, my God!" Joey said, gasping.

"You can imagine how valuable real estate is in the Quarter, especially in the location of Savannah's theater."

I turned to Clayton.

"I don't know what to say," I said.

"Why don't you boys take a bit to think about how you want to handle this. Remember, she wanted the two of you to have it because she loved you."

I looked over at Joey.

"We're going to have to talk this out," he said.

"I know," I said. "I know."

CHAPTER 13

❀

"You're shitting me," Katie said, over the phone.

She had flown back to San Francisco, but she called me many times throughout the day to check up on me. Her meeting with her parents had gone much better than she had expected. She even made plans to come back for the holidays. She said her parents had read some book written by Dr. Phil on parenting and had since decided to accept and embrace her daughter for the pink haired lesbian she was.

I called her right after my lunch with Mr. Radcliffe. Joey had to go meet an old friend from school, so we agreed to meet at the theater later that day to discuss.

"The whole business! She left it to me and Joey in equal shares," I said. "I don't know what to do, Katie. This one guy's offer to buy is huge. I could just focus on my own photography for a while, maybe open up a studio."

"What about Joey?" Katie asked.

"Well, it's certainly more than he'd make for a very long time as a social worker, and he mentioned in passing his desire to start a non-profit to promote HIV awareness in the African-American community."

"Sounds like a good deal for both of you. I'm sure your aunt would be happy that she helped make your dreams come true."

"I know …"

"But what, Mason Hamilton?"

"So much of Savannah is in that theater. It's her legacy, you know?"

"But she had been planning to sell it, right?" Katie pointed out.

"I know. I'm torn about the whole thing. I mean this whole trip has been …"

"It's a lot for you to take in, doll."

"At least Colin has stopped calling, and to be honest, he's been off my mind for a while now."

"Good. You're moving on from that," Katie said. "I'm sure whatever you and Joey decide to do will be the right decision."

"I hope," I replied.

"I'm getting a vibe," she said.

"A vibe about what?" I asked.

"That you may not be back in San Francisco for a period of time," she replied.

"You might be right," I admitted.

I heard her sigh on the other end.

"Will you be upset if that happens?" I asked.

"Honey, as long as you're happy. I'm *always* going to be just a phone call away. And now that I'm planning on visiting home more often, don't think you're getting rid of me!"

"I couldn't imagine life without your friendship," I replied.

"Joey!" I called out. I stood on the empty stage in Savannah's theater. It felt strange to see the place so still, so lifeless.

A huge spotlight came on right above my head scaring the shit out of me.

I jumped.

"Sorry," Joey said, coming from behind backstage. "I didn't mean to scare you, but look at that. I remember how to run the lightboard after all of these years."

"How was your lunch with your friend?"

Joey chuckled.

"Damn, it's been a weird day."

"Why? What else?" I asked.

"He offered me a job at an AIDS awareness organization here in New Orleans."

"Really? Wow!" I said.

"Yeah, that was another surprise," he said. He looked around the theater. "There's so much of Savannah here, isn't it? Hell, I practically grew up backstage. Drag queens were some of my first friends. Miss Althea used to bring me Elmer's candy every weekend."

"Savannah built such a sense of community here."

"I wonder what will become of all of the staff," Joey said.

"You mean if we sell?"

"Yeah," he answered. "It's a pile of money, isn't it?"

"More than I ever thought I'd see," I said.

My eyes roamed the walls of the theater at the framed posters-pictures of Savannah, her performers, her staff, patrons. I started to cry.

"Hey, hey," Joey said, walking over to me and putting his strong arms around me.

I began sobbing into his chest.

"I was so lucky to have her. My God, what would have become of me if it hadn't been for her?" I said.

"What about me, too? She became my surrogate mother after my mom died. If she hadn't swooped in …"

Joey lifted my chin and dried my tears with the back of his hand.

"Everyone here was lucky to have her," he said.

As we stared into each other's eyes, underneath the same spotlight I had first seen Joey under many, many years ago we both unexpectedly, but passionately, began to kiss each other.

When we both pulled back, we just looked at each other. Neither of us seemed to know what to say.

I finally broke the silence and said, "Whoa!"

"You can say that again," Joey replied. "Nice to know you're still a good kisser."

I giggled.

"You mean you remember after all of these years?"

"You bet," he said.

"I didn't have much practice back then, either."

"You were a natural," he replied, smiling.

I gave him a tight hug and a kiss on the neck.

"Joey?" I whispered into his ear.

"Yes?" he asked.

"You think we could actually make this work?"

"There's only one way for us to find out," he answered.

I knew both of us were talking about more than just the business.

"Maybe we should take some time before making any big decisions about this place. Take some time to weigh all of the options-for both of us," he said.

"I think that sounds like a plan," I replied.

Epilogue

Late August, 2005

I laid on the hotel bed in Jackson, Mississippi with Joey's arms around me after we had just made love to each other. Since we evacuated before the hurricane, we had spent the time listening to the radio or watching the news on the television non-stop.

Finally, Joey reached for the remote and turned off the television.

"Enough for right now," he said.

He took me into his arms, kissed me deeply, and comforted me in a way that only he could.

It was painful not knowing how our friends and staff were doing back in New Orleans. We had no idea if they all got out safely. We had no idea if the theater, which was as popular as ever under our management, was still standing or flooded out.

I just thank God that Joey insisted we leave at what turned out to be the very last minute we could evacuate. Otherwise, we could be amongst the thousands trapped in the Superdome or the convention center waiting for help that didn't seem to be arriving.

We packed up just a few precious belongings, pictures and such, and our little pug, Chi-chi, and took off. I think we may have gotten one of the last hotel rooms in Jackson.

Mother kept trying to insist that Joey and I come on up to her house-a couple of hours away. I told her if it looked like it would be a few days before we could go back to New Orleans, then we would go to her place. Both of us were anxious to go back and see whatever damage may be waiting for us. Chi-chi, pacing back and forth before sleeping next to the foot of the bed, was also going nuts in the hotel room.

I gave Joey a kiss and began to get out of the bed.

"Where are you going?" he asked.

"To see what food we have left," I answered.

Even the supermarkets in Jackson were practically empty of inventory. The storm was not nearly as bad there as in New Orleans, but the electricity had been out for almost a day.

Joey sat up and switched on the television.

"I thought you said we were done watching for awhile," I said, shaking my finger.

"I know. Sorry," he said.

He lifted the remote to turn off the television, but then an image caught my eye.

"Wait!" I said.

We both sat in front of the television beyond amazed.

The annual Southern Decadence festival had been planned for that weekend. Southern Decadence had a long history as the "gay Mardi Gras" that took place every Labor Day weekend. Tourists from around the world joined locals for what ended up being a weekend of fun, drinking, and debauchery. Katrina's wrath arrived just a few days before the festivities were to begin.

"Holy shit!" Joey said. "I don't believe it."

"Neither do I," I said.

On the television, a reporter stood in the middle of the French Quarter surrounded by around twenty people, dressed in traditional Southern Decadence costumes. There were people actually still celebrating Decadence amongst all of the horrible death and destruction. It was an act of strength and defiance that spoke volumes.

Both Joey and I started to cry and we held each other tight.

It felt like the first sign we had that New Orleans lived on and no matter how long it took, the city would survive.

I had a feeling that my Aunt Savannah's spirit was there with all of them, too. She was probably wearing one of her traditional short dresses and heels. I could see her in my mind holding her cocktail high in the air and saying, "Fuck you, Miss Katrina!"

I buried my head into Joey's chest. He embraced me even tighter. Despite being so far from our house, with Joey I always felt at home.

I thought that somehow everything would work out. We'd all be okay. That I had to believe.

978-0-595-42461-0
0-595-42461-9